The Billionaire's Choice Standalone Series

Paging Dr. Grumpy Billionaire

S.E. Riley

The Redherring Publishing House

Paging Dr. Grumpy Billionaire

Table of Contents

What is closed, holds the secret.

Prologue

Zoe

Estella Lawson was one of the kindest women I knew. And as I stood by the side of her grave, I thought about the first time I met her.

It had been another hot Summer fifteen years ago when I'd walked out into the backyard of my parent's house in Cañon City and saw a slight, willowy girl with olive-colored skin standing on the other side of the fence. *So, these must be our new neighbors,* I thought. I'd heard so much about the Italian family who'd just moved here from New York. I'd immediately run over to her and smiled my biggest smile, desperate to introduce myself.

"I'm Zoe!" I called. *"What's your name?"*

"I'm Giulia," replied the girl in her soft, lilting voice, which betrayed just a little of her Italian heritage. I was drawn to her shyness and her polite smile. And she was drawn to me, happy, smiley, silly Zoe. Within an hour, I'd gone round to their house, where we sat together under the porch by the backdoor as her mother prepared us fresh, homemade lemonade and asked me

about myself. I told her everything I could: that my family and friends were all from Cañon City, and my family had lived there for what seemed like forever. I also told her that I was looking forward to showing Giulia around.

Estella had beamed when I said that and kissed my forehead for the first time, as she would every time she saw me from then on. She stroked my head, saying, "bambina cara." *Dear girl.*

"And you meet Adriano, too!" she cried. *"Adrian,"* she said, correcting herself hastily as a look of fear passed behind her dark, brown eyes. *"ADRIAN!"* she cried. *"Come out and speak to your neighbor, Zoe!"*

Behind the screen of the backdoor, I saw a boy appear. Like his sister and mother, his skin was olive-toned, dark, black hair swept by the wind. He looked older than fourteen, the age which Giulia and I were. He was tall, even then, with wiry, athletic limbs and a strong, handsome face with high cheekbones. His eyes, too, were deep-set and soulful, brown with black pupils that spoke a thousand unsaid words. But the truth was, Adrian was different from Estella and Giulia. He was sullen and moody, strong-willed, and quick to anger. And it was clear from the moment we'd met that, however much he fascinated me, there was no amount of smiles, kind words, or cheery greetings that could make Adrian so much as grin at me. He was an incorrigible grump who, after only a few meetings, took to calling me "Glitter-girl." I held my head high and kept on being myself. *"Be yourself, Zoe,"* my mom would say. *"Everyone else is taken."* And so, I carried on smiling, even though as Giulia and I became best friends, Adrian and I became bitter enemies.

But now, here, beside the graveside, I looked up into those brown eyes of his, wishing I could reach out to Adrian. His face was closed to those around him, but I could see he was in pain—unbearable pain from losing his mother. Mystery had surrounded the Lawsons ever since they arrived in town. They'd moved to the USA when Adrian was three years old, and Giulia was a mere infant. I'd never discussed it with Giulia, but I knew there was so much that Estella had never gotten the chance to tell her children when, a week ago, she'd suffered a freak aneurysm.

As the casket was lowered into the ground, I held Giulia's hand in mine and pulled her to me as she wept. But my eyes stayed firmly fixed on Adrian across the graveside. And my head reeled with grief, concern, and guilty desire.

*

At the wake, later, I stood among the people. Our neighbors came and went, dressed in black, quietly chatting—stopping to share a fond memory of Estella or offer their condolences to their two children. A few less sensitive relatives congratulated Adrian on his recent accomplishments. After all, it wasn't very often that they were in the same room as someone who'd just been on the cover of TIME Magazine.

Adrian had been featured in a piece celebrating the country's youngest billionaires. At the age of twenty-three, while still in medical school, he and his friends invested in a solar energy company. The previous year, the stock had been valued and estimated at a thousand times its original value. Adrian had happily sold his shares, which amounted to well-over two billion dollars, and was now happily living off the income that came in from his massive portfolio, which was managed in New York. At the same time, Adrian impressively continued his career as a qualified surgeon.

It was kind of an amazing story, but he clearly wasn't in the mood to talk about it. Adrian had long since left Cañon City for his job at Johns Hopkins, and he'd caught a red eye to be at the funeral. He hadn't slept—that much was clear from the dark circles beneath his darker eyes—and I could only watch as he glowered at people who had wanted to talk to him.

"Where's Adrian?" I whispered to Giulia half an hour later, who was keeping her mind off things by tidying the buffet table.

"I don't know," she said anxiously, her eyes flitting around the room. "Zoe, can you find him for me?"

I nodded. I wandered around the ground floor for a bit, searching for him, but Adrian was nowhere to be seen. I looked up at the bottom of the staircase; surely he'd be up there.

I climbed the stairs as the chatter of voices below faded to nothing more than a low noise, punctuated softly by the sounds of creaking wooden boards crossed by dress shoes and heels.

The landing was dark. I didn't think Adrian would be up here without turning the lights on, but as I left, my eyes rested on the room at the far end of the landing. The room that had always been off-limits to me and Giulia when we'd been teenagers, hanging out in her house, discussing clothes, books, and boys. Adrian's room.

I walked up to the door. I could see it was open, a crack of light shining through the door. I pushed it open, and there he was.

Adrian was sitting on his bed, looking down at a photo. He looked up as I entered.

"Oh," he said. "It's you."

That was typical of Adrian. Though these days he was tall, handsome, and dark, with broad shoulders and strong, athletic arms, I knew he'd never look twice at a girl like me. He looked moodier and more miserable than ever. "What's the Glitter Girl doing up here?" he said bitterly.

"Don't call me that," I said. "You know I hate that." Adrian's special nickname for me sounded so spiteful whenever he said it. I wouldn't have minded the name—I considered it a compliment. Except I knew what it meant when Adrian said it. It meant: *you're shallow, and I don't like you.* No matter how much I never judged him for his dark mood or grim expression, he always judged me for my smiling, happy-go-lucky nature.

"Giulia sent me to find you," I said quietly, meekly. I felt shy around him, even now.

"Why?" he said, and there was a fire in his eyes as he stood. He'd removed his jacket and loosened his tie and top button just enough for me to see the beginning of the thread of hairs covering his chest. It was then that I realized that sometime in the last ten years when I hadn't been looking, the boy I'd met that hot Summer day at the house on Reger Road had become a man. They were going to sell this house now, Giulia told me. She'd be able to get a place near to me. *"Maybe we could be neighbors,"* I'd said. But with Giulia selling her mother's home, Adrian would be gone. He'd have nothing to connect him to Cañon City anymore.

"I'm sorry," I said. "I didn't mean to make you angry."

He sighed. "You didn't, Zoe. It's just the way I am. I've always been a grump, but this?"

He turned and looked out of the window. "No one expected this."

I stepped towards him. I don't know why. All my instincts told me to back away. But I could tell Adrian needed my help. And I wanted to give him that help. So, I stepped towards him, quickly, gently, making as little sound as possible, and lifted my arms around his neck. I pulled him towards me, even though my attempt was comical—he was almost a foot taller than me. I rested my head on his shoulder to let him know that he wasn't alone and would never be alone.

"I like you," I said. "I know you hate me, but I've always liked you. And I just want what's best for you. That's what Estella would have asked of me, if she'd...if she'd...had time."

And then, without meaning to, the happy-go-lucky girl had tears streaming down her face. And it was Adrian's turn to hold me, to wrap me in his strong embrace and comfort me all he could.

"Zoe..." he said. "*Bambina cara*," he whispered in Italian. The term his mother had saved for me. "Dear little girl." I felt so dear to him then, so close, closer than I'd ever felt before. For just a moment, I no longer felt like the annoying friend of his little sister that Adrian had had to suffer the presence of all his adult life. Instead, I felt like I was his equal, more than that, maybe. I felt like I belonged to him and him to me, and the sensation was intoxicating.

"Help me," he said, choking back sobs. "Help me forget, *cara* Zoe..."

And before I knew it, we were kissing.

I didn't know what I was doing. My emotions were out of control. So even though I knew it was wrong, that it wasn't what was best for me or for Adrian, I began to kiss back, slowly. While my hands reached up to his shoulders and down across his collarbone until they pressed gently against his chest, our lips pressed gently together. Slowly, Adrian began to wrap my hair in his hands, reaching into my loose, blonde locks and gently running his fingers around the base of my neck. I sighed with delight, my tears gone, lost and drowning in the dark passion that ached between us, years of unspoken thoughts and feelings all rushing out of us, longing for release on this sad, awful day.

It wasn't long before I'd sat down on the bed, and Adrian had joined me, where his hands began to search my body for some peace, some tranquility which only gave way to more heat, more lust in the tiny, stifling bedroom. While his hands cupped my breasts and squeezed gently, my sighs filled the air, and he bent his head to kiss my cheeks, my neck, and the top of my chest. Even as I castigated myself for doing this on the day of Estella's funeral, my hands began to work at his tie until it was gone, and then, slowly, to fumble for the buttons of his dress shirt, revealing the soft, smooth tan skin I'd always known to be there. I bent myself, undercutting him, and kissed his chest, and Adrian made soft moans of delight as though he'd finally given himself up to this moment, understanding, as he always should have, that there was no going back, that this was how things were between us, and this was how we'd always wanted them to be.

I stood up, knowing I had to reveal myself to him, knowing that if I waited any longer, I'd go mad with longing for him. I stood and stripped, reaching down to pull the black midi dress over my head in one swift movement. He stood and cradled my nervous body in his hands as my hair tumbled to my shoulders.

"You're...beautiful," he said, and my heart sang, desperate for his validation. If Adrian wanted anything from me, he could have it. I was his, right there and then. I kicked off my shoes quickly, sending them skittering across the floorboard of the room.

I thought what happened next would be brief, but it wasn't. For such a guilty, awful thing, it was slow and sweet as the rays of the sun as it passed from one horizon to the other. He lifted me in one quick movement and stretched me out on the bed he'd slept in as a teenager, a bed that had long been the source of my fantasies as we grew up together.

"Adrian," I said as his mouth began to explore my breasts and stomach, and I felt his fingers and thumbs wrap gently around my panties.

He gently shushed me and lifted them off, and I watched the long, straight line of my legs before he tossed them to the floor.

Adrian dived deep into the most secret place I'd ever known, between my legs, and I winced a little at his stubble as it scraped the inside of my thigh. But this minor discomfort gave way to delight when his tongue found my clit and moved gently, side-to-side, then in slow, lazy circles. Below us somewhere, the chatter of the wake, the movement of footsteps rumbled, was far in the distance like the sound of an approaching train. Neither of us cared. We were lost in one another's bodies, lost in one another's worlds. My heightened senses magnified the slightest sound Adrian made a thousand times.

He continued to lick me slowly until I felt a strange pressure surfacing in my body. I'd never had an orgasm before that day. All the boyfriends I'd had up to that point had been too impatient. It makes me feel ashamed to say it like I was getting off at the funeral or something. But in his skilled hands, it was the work of six or seven minutes of gentle caresses and the firm pressure of his tongue that made me explode for him, panting, breathing, a small cry escaping my mouth before, for modesty's sake, I clamped both hands to my lips to stop myself from shouting. My legs trembled, and I felt the contractions, dizzyingly strong, slowly coming to a halt.

Adrian had taken off his pants and climbed onto me. He didn't feel heavy like I'd anticipated, even though he was bigger than me, much stronger too. He supported his weight with ease and comfort, looking into my eyes with alertness and focus as I felt the head of his enormously hard cock part the lips of my pussy.

This was unlike anything I'd ever felt before, unlike any sex I'd had with the one or two tedious boyfriends that I'd had in my twenties. I was stunned by the size of him, the way he filled me and kept on giving, as he slid deeper inside the wet, dark warmth that I knew drew him into me. Once inside me, I pulled his head down and kissed him on his lips, face, cheeks, and eyes, while my hands reached down his back and under his unbuttoned shirt to press him closer and bring his manhood deeper inside of me.

Adrian began to thrust now, and it was fire, heat, and willful temptation, and all the things I'd been warned it would be, yet it was heavenly, wonderful, and peaceful. His slow, deep, gentle thrusts warmed me and made me, somehow, grow impossibly wet for him to allow his enormous manhood passage through me. And as he did, he reached up and took my wrists in his hands, where he pressed them to the covers. "Zoe," he whispered, "I want you, I want..."

"I'm on the pill," I replied, to let him know, though I knew I didn't need to, that there was no way this would stop until Adrian Lawson, my best friend's grumpy brother, a billionaire I only saw on the front of magazines, fucked me until he came for me, inside of me. And I wanted it, more than anything. I was desperate for him, and as I felt him thrust deeper and faster and come to his climax, my hands broke free of his grasp, reached up, and scratched his back while I begged him to release himself, to possess me, control me, completely...

When Adrian came, I saw stars, my inner walls clumping down hard. He grunted and sighed, not wanting to shout, not wanting to alert the unwitting guests downstairs that he'd finished with such power and strength that it was a minute before his cock had stopped pulsing and throbbing inside me. When it was over, he rolled off me. My legs shook from the second orgasm. His back to me, he looked at the wall for a long time.

After twenty minutes, or maybe an hour, I don't know which, Adrian got up, got dressed, and left. Without saying a word. I was there, sitting in the room, slowly pulling myself together, getting my clothes on. Shame was resounding through my head like a red mist descending.

How was I going to explain myself to Giulia? Could I? What would she say if she found out what we'd done? And what about

Adrian? Would I ever see him again? Would I ever have the chance to tell him what all this had meant for me?

I turned and saw the photo he'd been looking at when I came in. It was a framed photograph of his mother.

What have we done?

Chapter 1

Zoe

A year later

"Hello there, neighbor!"

I'd recognize that honey voice and those Italian vowels anywhere. And, for the thousandth time, I counted my lucky stars that I lived on the same street as my best friend in the whole world.

"Giulia!" I exclaimed and turned around, dropping my groceries on the porch. "Oh my God. How was it?"

As I stepped down from my porch to hug her, as I did every time we met, Giulia grimaced and shrugged. "Ugh, *men*." I giggled. "I swear, this time, I'm done with them for good!"

I couldn't help but find it funny. Every time I saw Giulia, she'd just been on some kind of date with "her dream guy." And yet, a few days later, they'd done something to bitterly disappoint her.

"Well, count yourself lucky," I said in reply. "After all, that's the third date you've been on this month. I haven't been on one since...well."

I'd never told Giulia what had happened between me and Adrian at their now-sold childhood home one year ago. I couldn't stand the thought of her knowing what had happened between me and her brother. Giulia was my best friend.

I still thought about Adrian, day after day. The rough, raw, animalistic sex had been mind-blowingly good. But afterward, a cloud of shame had descended on me...and Adrian. We hadn't spoken since then. Not that I'd be interested in speaking to such a grumpy, moody guy.

"I just don't get it, Zoe," replied Giulia. "You're gorgeous. You're smart. And you're so nice. Everyone is always telling me how sweet you are! It's crazy you can't get a nice, big, strong, handsome hunk of a guy...."

"Easy there, sweetheart." I laughed at how quickly Giulia's eyes had clouded over as she imagined the perfect guy. "Besides..." I said, "...I think the reason I can't get a man is because I'm *too* nice."

"What do you mean?" said Giulia, confused. She waved her arms dramatically as she stood in the driveway. "*Cara Zoe*, too nice to get a boyfriend? You're crazy."

I blushed when she called me that. Giulia had picked up the term of affection from her mother and liked to use it on me in all sorts of embarrassing places.

"It's true," I protested. "If you're a stone-cold ice queen, guys will fall over themselves trying to please you. They'll take you on dates, buy you flowers, take you on vacations..."

"Not the guys I date," huffed Giulia. "Bunch of cheap scumbags, mostly."

"But if you're nice, guys just treat you differently," I continued. "It's like they're not interested. Anyway, who cares about that? Do you have the day off?"

"Duh!" said Giulia. "School's out, Zoe. I don't work on weekends."

"Well, excuse me," I said, tongue-in-cheek. "I kinda forget that everyone else isn't a nurse."

Giulia and I had both gone to Denver after we graduated high school. After Giulia got her degree in English Literature, she became a teacher and worked at the local elementary school. I'd decided to train as a nurse. I felt like it was my job in life to help people. It was a bit of a shock to my dad when he heard that I didn't want to become a lawyer-turned-judge like he was, but eventually, my mom got him to come around. She was an administrator at the local hospital and told me that if I felt like I could make a difference, she'd help me. And my sunny disposition made me pretty good at my job. It helps to be optimistic.

I had a shift at the hospital in an hour. I checked my watch.

"Hey," I said. "Wanna come in and hang out for a bit?"

Giulia grinned and put her hands on her hips.

"Thought you'd never ask, bestie. Besides, I've got something to tell you."

"What is it?"

"Adrian's moving to Colorado."

"*What do you mean he's coming back?*" I blurted out without thinking twice.

Giulia looked at me, a little shocked by my tone.

"Zoe?" she said. "Are you okay?"

I shook my head. "Yeah, I'm fine," I replied, flashing her that trademark Zoe-Hollis smile. But Giulia was immune to my happy-go-lucky act. She narrowed her eyes a little.

"Did something happen between you two?" she said. "I mean,

I know you guys have never exactly been friends. Adrian's kind of a sourpuss."

"You got that right," I said. "Look, Giulia, it's great news. I'm happy you guys are going to be together."

"I think he feels bad about not being here when mom...you know," said Giulia, looking away. I reached out and rubbed her arm. A year on, she still mourned her mom's passing. Estella's death had hit us all hard. "Anyway..." She perked up. "When he called the hospital, they were thrilled. They rolled out the red carpet, actually. 'The billionaire doctor' and everything..."

"That's amazing!" I said. *I just wish someone at work had told me...*

Adrian was pretty well-known, especially since he'd been on Time Magazine. He regularly showed up in print, usually on lists with names like "World's Hottest Billionaires." I was confused, though. He'd secured an incredible fellowship at Johns Hopkins. What was a talented surgeon like Adrian going to do in Colorado?

"They haven't made the announcement yet," said Giulia. "But your mom probably knows. Didn't she tell you?"

"Nah," I said. "Mom's pretty tight-lipped about things. She doesn't want to give me any special treatment."

"Damn," said Giulia. "Definitely not Italian, then."

We laughed, but I was uneasy already. "Where's he living?" I said, trying to play it cool. Trying to seem like I wasn't anxious about my best friend's moody brother moving into our neighborhood.

"Well, he's got a place of his own..." said Giulia. I breathed a sigh of relief.

"...But it isn't ready yet," she finished. Damn. My heart rate was right back up there. "So, he's gonna stay with me for a week. He'll be here on Monday."

"I'm so happy for you, Giulia." I meant it. I knew she missed Adrian; having him back would be like the old days. Except, it wouldn't. Not really. Things had never been good between Adrian and me before, and I didn't see how they could be good now. I opened my mouth to say something like that to Giulia, and maybe I wanted to confess, there and then, get off my chest the guilty secret I'd been keeping for a year. But I couldn't because my doorbell was ringing.

"Oh, damn," I said. "Probably the mailman. I'll be back in a second, okay."

Giulia nodded, taking an enormous gulp of the coffee I'd made her.

I got up and went to the front door, my mind racing as I contemplated what it would be like to see Adrian again. Memories of the afternoon at the funeral passed through my mind, tiny little impressions and visions of passion. His hands enclosing my wrist as he kissed my neck, the feeling of my legs wrapped around his waist...

I reached the door and stopped, staring at the shadowy figure standing outside. Whoever it was, they were dressed in black. They certainly weren't the mailman. I opened the door and stopped, staring dumbly at the dark-haired man with smooth, olive-toned skin who stood in front of me.

"Adrian...?" I whispered, my eyes wide.

"No...I'm Wesley. Wesley Banks. I just moved next door and..."

I felt my cheeks get warm.

"My God," I moaned. "I'm so embarrassed. Come in, come in." I waved him in. "I thought you were someone else. I'm so sorry."

"Really..." said Wesley, smiling as he settled himself at my table, "...it's okay."

"So THIS is the new neighbor!" said Giulia. "I'm so excited to meet you!"

I'd seen the removal van arriving early that morning, but I didn't realize that the new occupant of the house between mine and Giulia's homes would be moving in so soon. Wesley Banks was tall and athletic, if a bit skinny. He smiled at us with dark eyes. I studied him as he sat, gratefully accepting the coffee. I wasn't being crazy. He did look a lot like Adrian.

"You..." said Giulia, "...must be Italian. Though your last name doesn't exactly fit."

Wesley smiled nervously. "Mum remarried when we moved to the States, and I took my stepdad's last name." He was pretty handsome. He had a pair of black cargo pants on and a long-sleeved black top. He grinned at us from behind wire-rimmed glasses.

"Oh, cool. Where did you move from?" My best friend leaned her elbow on the counter.

"I'm from California. I worked in Silicon Valley for a while but moved up here to take a software engineering job."

He didn't sound like he was from Cali. The softest hint of a foreign accent was there, though most people probably wouldn't notice it.

"Welcome to the neighborhood, Wesley," I said.

"Please," he replied. "Call me Wes."

Giulia smirked. "He's a charmer, isn't he?" she said. I groaned.

Don't start flirting with your neighbor, Giulia!

"So, what do you guys do for fun around here?" said Wes. "I've never been to Cañon before. And it's kind of hard to make new friends when you spend all day stuck at a computer."

"Well, don't you worry," Giulia purred. "*Cara Zoe* here is the friendliest girl in town. And the most well-connected. Her dad's a judge, and her mom's an administrator for the city hospital. And Zoe's a nurse, so if you get hurt..." Giulia burst into giggles when she said that. I rolled my eyes.

"I'll bear that in mind," said Wes, smiling. "Look, I stopped by to say hello and introduce myself, but I've got to go."

"Me too!" I said, looking at my watch. "I've got a shift at the hospital in half an hour. But look, maybe we could get together and do something nice soon?" My initial impression of Wes was that he was a kind, sweet, shy guy. He was handsome and polite, and it was clear he and Giulia would get along. I was clearly going to have to chaperone.

"It was really nice to meet you," he said on the porch.

"You too!" I said. "And, sorry again that I confused you with Giulia's brother, Adrian."

"Hey..." he said, "...if you were that excited to see him, he's a lucky guy."

After Wes had walked back across my yard and gone inside, Giulia practically fell on the floor.

"Oh my *GOD*," she cried, doubling over with excitement. "He was *totally* flirting with you."

"Oh, that's silly," I replied. Besides, I had enough to think about.

It wasn't too long before Adrian and I would be co-workers.

Chapter 2

Adrian

I've never been the happiest guy in the room but trust me, I was worse without my morning coffee.

I heard a knock at the door as I looked forlornly at the hospital reports on my screen.

I sighed and pinched my brow. I checked my watch. 8.00 am. Who could it be?

"Come in," I said and closed the screen where I'd been reviewing the stats for the previous quarter on the ward.

The door opened, and in stepped Megan Hollis. Make no bones about it: ninety-nine percent of hospital administrators were interfering busybodies who didn't know a damn thing about medicine. Megan Hollis was in that one percent.

"What can I do for you, Megan?" I said.

"Working late, Adrian?" she said, grinning. "Or, working early?"

I grimaced. "Both, actually," I huffed. "I couldn't sleep, so I've been reviewing patient statistics in my sister's kitchen all morning. I got in about half an hour ago."

"How is Giulia?" She'd always been so fond of my younger sister.

"Good," I said, "I think. It's been pretty hard since my mom's passing. But we've pulled through together. It's nice to be here for her."

"Have you spoken to Zoe yet?" A knot inside my stomach clenched a little tighter. *Oh great*, I thought. I hadn't even remembered that Glitter Girl worked here until I'd told Giulia.

"Actually, I haven't seen her since the funeral," I said. *The funeral, where we had crazy, passionate sex in my childhood bedroom, not two hours after I'd buried my mother.* I was going to have to watch myself around Megan and her 'adorable' (read: annoying) daughter.

"I'm sure she'll be happy to see you again," said Megan. "Now, Adrian, I want to talk to you about today. We're not a bad hospital, but as you'll know, if you've been reading our stats this morning, we could be doing a lot better. And a large part of our decision to hire a teaching fellow from Johns Hopkins was based on changing that."

"You sure it wasn't just because I'm famous?" I muttered. All my working life, people have assumed that I'm a fake. They hear the name, see the media coverage of my story, and think I'm only halfway confident. That is, until they see me in an operating room, performing complex cardio surgery. Or managing a busy trauma ward. It hasn't exactly helped me work on my personality.

Megan laughed politely. "No, it wasn't, Adrian. Though that is important. You're our new public face. We're keen to work on a strategy for improving the public standing of this hospital. And I'd like you to conduct a full inspection of the cardiology and intensive care wards today."

I sighed, feeling the red mist descend. I was already booked in for *two* surgeries. And requests for private consultations were already starting to pile up. Once Cañon City's wealthier residents had heard The Billionaire Doctor was about to start working at the hospital, of course, they'd all been clamoring to see me.

"I know it's a lot," said Megan. "But we need this. The photographer is waiting downstairs. Just let him know when you're ready to go."

"The photographer?" I exclaimed. "You're kidding."

"I wish. The rest of the board of directors have already decided. They want you in the paper, on the hospital website, newsletters..."

I stood, giving an open drawer in my desk a desultory kick to shut it.

"Well, no time like the present," I said, taking off my jacket and putting on a white coat.

*

"It would be a little better if we could see you up close and personal with the patients," said Marty, the photographer. He was a sweet enough kid, maybe nineteen years old.

"I bet it would," I replied and flashed him a look. My eyes were dark and deep brown, and one thing I knew about myself was that I had a pretty intense stare. With my Nikon-toting friend cowed, I made my way to the end of the corridor.

"This is just absolutely classic," I said, lifting my clipboard and making a note. As I did, I heard the irritating clicks of a camera shutter behind me. The dull, tasteless cappuccino I'd sipped at five minutes ago had done nothing to quell my caffeine withdrawal. "Tito! Next time you stack the medicine trolley, I want the SSRIs and the tranquilizers stacked in different compartments, okay?"

"But, Doctor," said Tito, shrugging his shoulders. "Takes too long, no?"

"Takes too long?" I snarled. "Do you know how many hospital-located medical incidents are due to maladministering medications?"

"Malad...what?" replied Tito.

"*Sixty-seven percent*," I said. "Tito, stack the medications properly. Or I'm not going to be so nice next time."

"Damn," I heard a nurse whisper as I walked out of intensive care. "That was him being *nice*?"

For a hospital in a small town without much of a budget or resources, Cañon City was a pretty good place. I was being deliberately stern. I wanted it run like the doctors were fresh-faced, eager graduates from med school and like the nurses were bright-eyed, bushy-tailed newbies who were unjaded by years of service. I would show them that there was more to The Billionaire Doctor than a nine-figure bank balance.

We took a lift down to cardiology. It was my primary specialism when I trained as a surgeon. The way the heart worked had always fascinated me. A living, pulsing organ responsible for conducting blood throughout the body. Livers repaired themselves, and a significant proportion of us were missing a kidney and didn't even know it. But the heart? It needs to be healthy and well-functioning for you to live a good life. I looked after mine with plenty of swimming and running.

As we got down to the cardiology ward, I stepped into a welcoming committee. They must have been paged and told to expect me.

"Dr. Frisk?" I asked. "Adrian Lawson." I shook his hand. Ronald Frisk was pushing sixty, but he was spry for his age, slim and tall, and he showed no signs of retiring.

"Heard you were coming to give me a slap on the wrist," he said, grinning. I shook my head.

"It's a publicity op," I said quietly, pointing at the photographer. "Nothing more."

He nodded and shook his head. "I'm doing my rounds right now," he said. "Fancy joining me?"

"Love to." I relished the chance to do some actual medicine. I was starting to worry that Megan Hollis would only let me look handsome for the cameras.

As we entered the ward, I motioned to the kid with the camera to stay out. He slunk behind the automatic doors of the first room, trying to stay out of the way of the nurses and orderlies buzzing past. We came to the first bed. A woman lay beneath the sheets. She wrestled herself up onto her pillows and folded her arms.

"Eleanor May, 58," he said. "Eleanor's just had a triple bypass."

"Myocardial infarction on June 9th," I said. "How are you feeling, Eleanor?"

"Be a lot better if I could *leave*," she said, cantankerously. "Dr. Frisk here insists on keeping me."

I grinned. "I'm sure," I replied. "Unfortunately, Eleanor, when patients' hearts start to die on them, we do tend to recommend a longer stay."

"My heart's just fine," said Eleanor, giving a small cough. I noticed it with some suspicion. "Just a small, uh, *infraction*," she said casually.

"*Infarction*," I countered. "Do you know what that is, Eleanor?"

"Something to do with flow or something..."

"Yup," I said, "It's when blood flow to the coronary artery is prevented. It causes your heart muscle to begin to die. It's aggravated by smoking."

"I don't smoke!" she said.

"Judging by that cough," I replied, "you certainly do. That cough indicates you've been smoking sometime in the last three weeks—otherwise, your lungs wouldn't be in tar. I'd imagine they're under her pillow," I said to Dr. Frisk.

"This is low, even for you, Eleanor," he said, smiling thinly at her. Eleanor May looked like she'd been caught sneaking out late as a teenager. I reached under her pillow, and my hand emerged, holding a half-empty box of Lucky Strikes. "If you'd like to live any longer, Eleanor," I said, "I hope you won't mind if I take these. Hey! Marty!" I said.

The photographer appeared from behind the door, sheepish and embarrassed.

"Throw these in the trash, would you?" I said, tossing him the pack of Lucky Strikes.

"Having fun bossing people around?" said a familiar, sugar-sweet voice from behind me.

I groaned and gritted my teeth, and turned around.

"Zoe Hollis," I said. "How long's it been?"

"Good morning, Dr. Lawson," replied Zoe.

It had been a year since we'd seen each other, but she hadn't changed a bit. Zoe was still her same old self. Her gorgeous blonde hair that usually tumbled about her shoulders was done up in a ponytail. I didn't think looking attractive in blue scrubs was possible, but she somehow managed it. They matched her soft sea-blue eyes that were glowing under the ward's artificial lighting. Zoe had never been skinny, but her figure still drew my eye, her ample breasts and curving hips practically beckoning me. Flashes of that day came back to me.

"You two know each other?" said Dr. Frisk.

"We grew up together," said Zoe. "We were neighbors. I guess we are again, now."

"Hello there, Zoe," I said dryly. "Done any work yet today? Or are you still more interested in reading Jane Austen to the patients?"

Ronald Frisk chuckled. "Around here..." he said, "...we think of Zoe as the team mascot. She's always doing her best to keep the patients happy."

"Clearly not doing enough to keep them healthy," I quipped. "Did you know about Mrs. May's smoking?"

Zoe rolled her eyes. "Her husband brings them in for her on Tuesdays and Thursdays when he visits," she said. "I'll make him hand them over from now on. You know, since we're living in a dictatorship now."

"Just trying to protect my patient's health is all," I replied. "Though, perhaps you think you should be in charge. Since your mom's running the show around here."

Frisk was trying to see the funny side, but there was nothing funny at all about Glitter Girl trying to show me up in front of another doctor. Or in front of the hospital staff. I was so used to seeing Zoe smiling and cheerful that I was surprised when a look of annoyance flashed over her mouth.

"Maybe Dr. Lawson doesn't appreciate me trying to cheer up

some patients..." she said, "...but the scientific community does. After all, wasn't there an article in the American Journal of Cardiology you were telling me about last month, Dr. Frisk, about laughter and heart health?"

"You're right, Zoe," said Frisk, nodding.

"I guess if laughing really is good for your heart, I wouldn't be surprised if Dr. Lawson ended up as a patient in here before long," she said, smiling sweetly. "After all, I haven't seen *him* smile since the day we met."

Marty, who was standing by the doorway, giggled.

"I don't have time to stand here getting insulted all day," I said. "I have surgery in forty-five minutes."

"Okay, Zoe, I think that's enough," said Frisk. "Let's show Dr. Lawson the rest of the ward—"

Zoe opened her mouth, probably to deliver another barb, but then the senior nurse called her over.

"Zoe!" she said. "Can you help me with something? We need to check on Mr. Deandre's levels."

She stood for a moment. I could practically see the steam rising from her body. A smug satisfaction came over me for a second. Then in a flash, she turned on her heels and left. Something in me growled to see her go. I wanted to call her back, to make her stay and listen to me tell her how much of an irritating person she was. I was seething with anger. No one, especially not Zoe, had a right to talk to me like that!

But then she was gone. I pressed a finger to my temple.

I was getting a headache.

Chapter 3

Zoe

"Giulia!" cried Wes. "You're getting it on my shirt!"

Giulia fell down, laughing. Adrian had been working at the hospital for one week. I'd had the day off on Saturday and had decided to repaint my bedroom. Giulia had offered her help, and I'd gratefully accepted—her house wasn't exactly the easiest place for me to be now that Adrian had arrived.

I like to give people the benefit of the doubt, but there's no denying it...Adrian was acting like a jerk. He was arrogant, strict, and impossibly moody to work with. His surgeries were amazing. Doctors and trainees at the hospital were talking about him in hushed breaths. But he was making my days and nights in the cardiology ward a total nightmare.

"*Why isn't this clean?*" he'd say. "*Why isn't that chart filled out?*"

And every time, I had to do what grumpy Dr. Lawson told me.

He was even trying to crack down on the time I spent cheering up the patients by reading to them or talking with them. He was a killjoy, always bringing down the patients with stern warnings about their health habits or grim diagnoses.

I wouldn't mind so much if he were unremarkable. I'd just think Adrian was an asshole doctor. I knew how to deal with them. But his presence scrambled my brains. On the one hand, he was a mean jerk. On the other hand, you didn't meet many doctors who drove a Maserati to work each morning! Adrian was handsome, good-looking, and talented at his job. So far, he hadn't mentioned our secret, either. And I was determined to keep it that way.

So, I was happy that Giulia showed up that Saturday morning, armed with three tins of paint and some brushes, with Wesley in tow, looking meek but excited. I didn't mind Giulia bringing Wes along, even if I was hoping for us to have some girl time to ourselves. Wes was being really nice.

While I worked with a small brush, doing detail, they were busy rolling wide swathes of paint onto the wall of the house. I'd bought this place just last year but had never gotten around to fixing it up. When Giulia bought the house two doors down, we promised to help each other make our dream houses.

"You guys grew up next door to each other, and now you live on the same road?" said Wes. "I can't believe it!"

"We've been friends since, like, the first day I moved here," said Giulia. "I mean, how could you not be friends with Zoe? You know what my older brother calls her?"

"*Don't*, Giulia!" I said. I still wasn't sure I knew Wes well enough to spill all of my secrets, especially not the embarrassing, demeaning nickname Adrian had bestowed on me as a teenager.

"What is it?" said Wes. He was really curious. I started to wonder if Giulia might be right about Wes having a little crush on me.

"Can I tell him, Zoe?"

I balked but sighed.

"Come on!" said Wes. "Tell me!"

"It's Glitter Girl!" said Giulia. I felt my cheeks burn.

"Because I'm a happy-sparkle-sunshine kind of girl," I said apologetically.

"Hey," said Wes, "I'm not one to judge. Most software engineers don't exactly win the popularity score at high school."

"Well, Adrian's pretty nerdy, but he was still popular at school," said Giulia.

"Yeah?" said Wes. "Tell me about him! He's kind of interesting, right? Isn't he famous?"

I snorted. I didn't think very much of Adrian's fame—or at least, I pretended not to.

"Well, the first thing you need to know about Adrian is that he had a huge crush on Zoe," said Giulia.

"Oh, he did not," I said.

"How do you know?"

"Well..." explained Giulia, "...remember that time you asked Mike Brenshaw to prom?"

I was practically in agony at the memory. "God, don't remind me," I said. "High school sucked."

Giulia snorted. "He was so mean. He told you he'd never want to go with you, not in a million years. And remember, Zoe has always been this pretty and this nice. It was crazy."

"He reduced me to tears," I said. "I think I got sent home early that day."

"Right. So, anyway," continued Giulia. "That evening, Adrian tells me he's going over the bridge, which is where Mike used to live. He comes home an hour later, looking mad as hell. The next day…" she said, with bated breath, "…Mike Brenshaw came into school, apologized to Zoe, gave her flowers and chocolate, and offered to take Zoe to prom. Can you believe it?"

"No way!" said Wes. "Is that true?"

I nodded and showed the faintest hint of a smile. "As I recall, I told him I wouldn't. Not in a million years."

"He must really like you," said Wes.

"It…it was years ago," I said. "Anyway, you should see how things are with us now. Dr. Frisk says he's going to have to talk to my mom if we don't stop fighting!"

"You guys don't get on?" said Wes.

I looked at Giulia, who was still busy covering the wall in the lovely shade of yellow she'd picked out for me. I didn't want to say anything bad about her brother in front of her. But the truth was Adrian and I were fast becoming sworn enemies on the ward. I couldn't stop myself from answering back to him.

There was a knock at the door. "I'll get it!" said Giulia. She ran downstairs.

There was an awkward silence in the room with Wes and me.

"So, how come Adrian and Giulia have the surname Lawson? If they're from Italy, I mean?" said Wes as he continued to paint.

I felt a little offended that he wasn't going to ask me anything about myself. Not that I expected to be the center of attention. But Giulia thought Wes would ask me on a date pretty soon, and I didn't know how I felt about that. I didn't think he would, honestly. But if he did…what would I say? I tried not to overthink it.

"They changed it when they came to the States," I explained.

"Adrian's dad was...well, I don't really know anything about him. Estella—Giulia's mom—never talked about Italy much. I don't know."

"What was Estella's last name?" said Wes.

That was a weird question to ask. I turned to look at him. Wes sat there on his haunches, painting the wall. Looking...normal, I guess.

I could hear complaining and snatches of Italian coming from downstairs. I rolled my eyes and applied thin, delicate lines of paint around the skirting board.

"It's just for a second," I heard Giulia say.

It was Adrian.

I could feel him come into the room. I didn't look up or stop what I was doing. I didn't want to give him the satisfaction.

"Sorry for dropping in like this," Adrian said. "My darling sister has locked the garage, and I need to get my car." His voice was deep and masculine, but it had sweetness, too. The truth was, hearing him talk like that made me weak at the knees. But I pulled myself together.

"Why didn't you just take a cab?" I said. "It's not like you can't afford it, is it?"

I was so busy feeling happy teasing him that I didn't realize something else was happening until I turned around and saw Wes. The paintbrush was still in his hand, but he was just standing there, with his arms by his sides. Standing and staring at Adrian.

I compared them, standing there. They were similar. Same height. But Adrian was stronger, with a barrel chest and long arms.

"Hi," said Adrian, a little awkwardly.

"Hi," said Wes. "Hi. How are you doing?"

"Fine, thanks," said Adrian. "You're Wesley, right?"

This was their first time meeting? But Giulia had been dragging Wes all over town. It was crazy that she hadn't introduced them yet.

"Boy," said Wes, looking at his phone. "It's getting kind of late. I should go back. I have to go grocery shopping and run some errands."

"Oh," said Giulia, disappointed. "Does that mean I'm gonna have to do this wall by myself?"

"Sorry, Giulia," said Wes, chuckling. "Maybe another time."

He put his roller in the paint palette and walked past Adrian, who just stood there.

"He's a little strange, isn't he?" said Adrian after we heard the door slam shut.

"Actually..." I said, "...he's really nice."

"Who? Wes?" said Giulia as she picked up both rollers in her hands and began to slather paint onto the walls at a ferocious speed. "How can you say that, *Adriano*? You're so rude sometimes, I swear."

Adrian shrugged. "Just seems a little awkward, that's all."

I ignored his cruel comments. "What do you want, Adrian?"

"As I've said, Zoe," he said sweetly, "I'd like the keys to the garage."

"Oh," replied Giulia. "Sure." She looked in her pocket. "Oh, damn," she said. "I must have left them in the house. Zoe, can you show Adrian where the spare key is?"

"Me?" I said. *Why me?*

"Yes, you! Is there another *Cara Zoe* in the room? I'm painting here!" said Giulia. "This is art. Like the Sistine Chapel. Michelangelo, coming through!" she said, veering past me with the rollers in her hands.

*

We walked in silence across Giulia's yard. "If that guy Wes is weird to you..." said Adrian, "...say something, okay?"

"What do you mean, *weird*? The only person being weird here is you," I said derisively.

"I don't know. He just gave me a strange feeling, is all."

"Well, don't say that around Giulia. She likes him. I like him."

"God," replied Adrian. "You're such a cinnamon roll. All squishy and sweet inside."

"I prefer the term 'positive person,'" I snapped back. "We can't all be walking around like a storm cloud."

"Jeez. You sound like my mother. God rest her soul."

"Good. Being compared to Estella Lawson is a compliment."

"Being compared to Wesley Banks, less so," quipped Adrian.

I cringed. *Giulia had told him what happened!*

"Do you *really* think we look similar..." said Adrian, "...or do you just have a type?"

I wanted to scream at him but decided, for once, to be the better person. "She keeps the key under this one," I said, lifting the second of a collection of potted plants Giulia kept by the side of her house.

"Thanks," said Adrian. "You can go back now."

But I didn't, much as I hated him. I stood there while he unlocked the garage door.

The door lifted. "Zoe," he said. "I don't like the way things are between us."

I smiled at him. *Finally, some maturity!*

"No? How would you like them to be?" I asked.

"It would be nice if we could just...forget...certain things that have happened," he said, swinging his hand on the garage door to throw it up into the rafters. He was strong. I could see his biceps under the t-shirt he was wearing.

What did Adrian mean by that? Did he want to forget what happened at the funeral? Or did he mean we should forget all the arguments we had?

I was about to ask him, but then I turned and saw the car.

"Oh my God," I said.

"What the hell?" said Adrian. Every muscle in his body was suddenly tense. He stomped forward, his face growing red.

"Who did this?" he said. He turned and looked at me.

I didn't know what to say. "I...I..."

"Was it you?" he said, his eyes aflame.

"NO!" I yelled. "You psycho, of *course* I didn't do this."

Why would he think I'd do anything like this?

Adrian was going to need to call a cab after all. The window of his car was smashed, and someone had keyed the bonnet, dragging metal across it in a jagged spiral. I stared at the scratched metal and tiny, sparkling shards which littered the bonnet. Someone had taken a can of spray paint and traced three letters on the side of the car.

Chapter 4

Adrian

Detective Vance was a stocky, balding man of about fifty. He had a confident, cocksure presence as he sat at his desk, leaning back in an enormous leather armchair.

"Well, Dr. Lawson. Haven't ever had anyone famous in my office up until now. I'm sorry we had to meet like this."

"That's quite all right, Detective," I muttered. I was still glowering with rage at whoever had taken it upon themselves to trash my car. "I'm just hoping you can catch this guy."

Vance nodded. "Trouble is, catching whoever did this can be pretty hard. Probably just teenagers."

"Teenagers?" I said. "Don't you think that's a little unlikely?"

Vance looked at me quietly for a moment and then chuckled. "Well, I didn't realize you were an expert in policing as well as medicine. Come on then, Mister Lawson. You tell me why it couldn't have been teenagers. After all, I'd usually put it down to youthful hijinks in a simple case of vandalism like this."

"Hijinks wouldn't require breaking into a house," I said

quietly. "If the car had been left parked on the street, I'd understand. It was in a secure, well-populated neighborhood behind a heavy metal garage door with an electric lock. Whoever did this probably broke into the house to reach the garage, wouldn't you say? The door would have shown signs of damage otherwise."

Vance made a face and nodded. "Could be. It certainly could be. But who on earth would want to get at you, Dr. Lawson?" He smiled. "Haven't made any enemies here in Cañon City, have you?"

I shook my head. "Nope."

"Got any enemies elsewhere? New York, maybe?"

I thought about it. My mother had brought us to New York when we first came to America, and we'd lived there in Queens until I was fifteen or sixteen. But I shook my head for a second time. "I trade in some stocks out there, but I don't spend much time in the city anymore."

Vance stared into the distance. I got the feeling he wasn't expecting to find the culprits who'd vandalized my car. I got the feeling he didn't care much at all.

"Well, I'll provide what information I can to the insurance company…" he said, "…if you forward me their details. The doors to the house and garage were locked, so you should be able to claim."

"I don't care about the insurance," I said. I could feel my temper getting the best of me. "I care about finding whoever's threatened me and entered my sister's house."

"Well, now," said Vance. "That's a pretty big accusation, wouldn't you say? After all, we don't know if anyone's threatening you."

"Someone wrote 'DIE' on my car!" I exclaimed, leaning forward in my chair.

"A car they may not even know belongs to you."

"Who else owns a Maserati in this neighborhood?" I was beginning to feel furious.

"Easy now, Adriano."

I looked at him. "Adrian," I said. "Please."

Vance smiled. "Sure. Adrian, please be calm. I understand this is upsetting. But I will do what I can. I just need your complete cooperation."

"Understood."

"At the minute, there aren't enough details for me to point to any probable suspect. But there is one thing I know," said Vance.

"What's that?"

"Lawson, that's...that's not an Italian name, is it?"

"My mother changed it when we moved here," I replied.

Vance nodded again and made a note of it. "Well. Anything else?"

*

"Anything else?" said Giulia. "That's what he said? *Anything else?*"

I nodded. "It's a crock," I said. "But it doesn't matter. I'll be out of here in three days when the house is ready."

Zoe was sitting at the kitchen table next to Giulia. I could tell my sister had been crying. The incident had really upset her. She, like me, knew that whoever had done this had gotten into the house.

"Did you find your key?" I inquired.

Giulia nodded, sniffling. "It was on the kitchen countertop," she said.

"Funny," said Zoe.

"What's funny about this, Zoe?" I snapped. "I can't wait to hear the bright side."

She looked at me with contempt. "I just think it's odd..." she continued, "...because it isn't like Giulia to leave her house key behind."

"What are you even saying?" I said. "That someone stole Giulia's key. Who?"

"I don't know!" she said. "But I wish you'd listen to me instead of shouting—"

"And I wish...." I said, as I stormed out of the kitchen, "...that you'd leave my family *alone*."

As I went up the stairs, I could hear Giulia start to sob quietly again.

*

The following day, I was on a shift at the hospital. It was the usual: things weren't exactly swimmingly at Cañon City Hospital. But I was beginning to feel more settled in the pace, and slowly I began to realize that it was because of the camaraderie between the staff, the kind you don't get in a big teaching hospital like Johns Hopkins.

There was just one problem, though. I had to do my rounds on the cardiology ward in a few minutes. And I knew who'd be waiting for me when I got there. Zoe.

I hadn't been wrong about her. She really was a ray of sunshine. Over the past week, patients have told me stories about their interactions with Zoe. A fourteen-year-old kid who was going to need a transplant: Zoe had brought him his favorite kind of cookies from the store when she found out he didn't like the food in the hospital. We'd had to transfer the kid out to a specialist unit where they could look after him, but he'd left happy and optimistic.

Oh, then there was Mrs. May. Zoe had gotten her *nicotine patches*. She realized the old woman wouldn't quit just because I told her.

There was something I didn't want to admit to myself yet, something about how she looked after people on the ward, and it made me jealous to think about. *Jealous? Me?*

Quietly, I left my office, slipping on my lab coat and grabbing an iPad.

I paced down the corridor, looking for her. I didn't see her. I made my rounds with a 1st-year resident surgeon, Greg, talking to everyone. All of them said the same thing. *I don't feel any different. Much the same today, doc. Zoe was a big help, however.*

"I think that's enough for today," I told Greg. "Get yourself home."

We'd pretty much covered everybody except for an elderly patient in Room 2. This was a private room. I checked the notes. Mr. McCabe. Suffering from angina, he'd been brought in a few days ago. No friends or family had visited yet.

I went to the room, where I saw that the curtains were closed. It was late in the day, and the rooms on that side of the hospital didn't get a lot of light after 3 pm. The lamp was on, and behind the curtains drawn around the bed, I could see a familiar silhouette by the bed.

It was Zoe.

She was reading to him.

"You are part of my existence, part of myself," she read, holding up the book. "You have been in every line I have ever read since I first came here, the rough common boy whose poor heart you wounded even then."

I recognized it immediately. It was Dickens. Why was she reading Dickens? Her voice was soft and a little lower than it usually was. I stood in the doorway, listening, a faint smile playing on my lips. She was a sweetheart to spend time with the old man like that.

"You have been in every prospect I have ever seen since...on the river, on the sails of the ships, on the marshes, in the clouds, in the light, in the darkness, in the wind, in the woods, in the sea, in the streets. You have been the embodiment of every graceful fancy that my mind has ever become acquainted with."

I coughed gently to let her know she wasn't alone. Zoe sprang up, pulled back the curtains with a happy, heartfelt smile—

Then, she saw it was me.

"Oh," she said. "It's you. Dr. Lawson, this is..."

"Mr. McCabe, right?" I said. "How are you feeling today?"

"Just fine, thanks, doc," he said. "Especially since this lovely young lady started to read to me."

"Glad to hear it," I said. "I think we're going to get started tomorrow. There shouldn't be a need for surgery. You've had a close call, but if you change your diet and adopt some exercise, it should prevent you from deteriorating."

"That's good news," said Mr. McCabe. But it seemed like he'd been cheered up by good news long before I got there.

"My shift's over now, Doctor," said Zoe. "Is Jenny here yet?"

"Sure," I said. "Can...can I talk to you before you go?"

She rolled her eyes, no doubt expecting a harangue about something. "Yeah."

Zoe stepped out into the corridor, said goodbye to the old man, and shut the door.

"Is reading Charles Dickens part of your usual duties?" I said, smiling at her.

"I'm just trying to be useful," said Zoe. "I got everything else done. The logs, the medication. The trolley's been cleaned up. We're looking good. I was just—"

"I'm not lecturing you," I said. She stopped and looked at me. Those enormous blue eyes opened momentarily, threatening to swallow me whole.

"You're not."

"No," I said. "I'm a scientist, Zoe. I do what the evidence tells me. And the evidence tells me that people get better when you're around. At least they feel better. That's half the battle, isn't it?"

"This doesn't sound very scientific of you," muttered Zoe.

"I want to apologize," I said. "I had no right to tell you to leave us alone. You're Giulia's best friend. And even if we don't see eye-to-eye about anything, and even if there's...history, I'm humble enough to admit that you do a lot of good around here. And I'd like you to keep doing good."

Zoe looked at me suspiciously as though she were expecting this to be some kind of trick. But it wasn't. I meant every word.

"Thank you for saying that, Adrian," she said. "I want you to know that..."

I waited to hear it.

She didn't say anything. "Never mind."

Zoe said goodnight and walked out of the ward.

I didn't tell her how pretty I thought she was or how the sound of her voice made me long for the day when she'd met me in my room and we'd tumbled into bed.

I didn't tell her that I longed to kiss her, there and then.

I didn't tell her that fire overtook me when Zoe Hollis walked in a room, that half the time when we were arguing, I wanted to be tearing her clothes off and taking her.

Remind me why I didn't tell her that?

Chapter 5

Zoe

The following day, after Adrian spoke to me in the hospital and I rushed home, knees weak and heart beating faster than I ever knew it could, I got an envelope in the mail. I recognized the elegant, old-school handwriting and tore it open.

It was an invitation.

"Adrian Lawson requests the pleasure of my company at his housewarming party," I read. Okay, so I'd been expecting some kind of secret love letter. What can I say? I'm an old romantic. But I was delighted to see he'd personally written on mine with a pen.

Zoe,

A chance to have some fun and enjoy life for a bit. Hope you'll come. You can get a ride with Giulia and Wes xxx

A.

I spent the next two days at work, staying out of his way. In the meantime, the whole town was chattering about the party. No one had seen Adrian's finished house yet, but it was pretty famous. A local historic site, Cañon Lodge had been one of the few mansions built in the City by a retired oil baron who liked the hot climate. It seemed like half the town had been invited because things were already buzzing by the time we got there on Saturday night.

Cañon Lodge was behind an electronic gate at the top of a hill. Wes gave me and Giulia a lift in his car. He seemed to have recovered from his attack of shyness in front of Adrian. "I can't wait to party with you guys!" he said.

"This is gonna be so much fun," said Giulia. "When Adrian throws a party, it's pretty crazy."

"Would you get a look at the place!" I said, and Wes and I looked out the window in disbelief.

It was an amazing sight, a gleaming white building in Second Empire style, with steps leading up an enormous porch with a curved roof. Up above it, in a clump of terracotta roofing, stood a tower stretching up like the layers of a wedding cake.

"That's incredible," I said. "Wow, he must really be into the playboy lifestyle."

"Not as much as you'd think," replied Giulia. "But he sure can pretend when he wants to."

Out front on the paved driveway, a valet took the car and parked it for us. We climbed the steps of the porch. Music came from behind the house, which I could hear now—faint but with an insistent, four-to-the-floor beat. I began to get excited.

"Do you have your invitations?" asked a man at the door. He

44

was almost comically tall. We showed our cards to him, and he nodded and opened the front door.

Inside I could see people standing in the low, moody lighting of the enormous foyer. In the corner, I saw my parents and ran over.

"Hi, Mom," I said and kissed her on the cheek.

"Zoe, darling," she said. "You look so pretty today!" I'd dressed my best in a trademark yellow sundress with a pair of Penelope Chilvers slippers I was saving for a special occasion.

"Thanks, momma," I said. My dad reached over and embraced me.

"How's my little girl?" he said. "You look tired, sweetheart. They aren't working you too hard, are they?"

I smirked. "Dad, I'm a nurse," I said. "We're, like, the most overworked people in the world."

"Not that you'd know it from how Zoe works," Adrian said behind us. "She makes the job look easy."

I turned around. Adrian was...smiling. Like, actually smiling at me. "What's gotten you in such a good mood?" I said.

Adrian looked thoughtful. "Not sure," he said. "But it's definitely good timing. After all, can't have the host of a party being miserable and morose, can you?"

"You are *not* morose, Adrian," said my mother imperiously. "Just melancholic. It's a sign of a truly intelligent mind when one is disappointed by the world."

"Mom!" I said. My mother says the most depressing things at times.

"I think it's more intelligent to be optimistic, myself," countered my dad.

"That's nice, dear," said my mom dismissively. "Now, Adrian, tell us. Is Zoe giving you trouble? We're aware she's not the most conventional nurse on the ward."

I flashed Adrian a glance. He was dressed impeccably in a royal-blue tuxedo, flaunting his frankly exceptional physique. Our eyes met, and I thought I saw the hint of something other than his usual distaste for my cheerful personality in them.

"Actually," he said, "I'm coming round to Zoe's way of doing things. Imagine her kindness combined with my knowledge. We'd be an incredible duo." He put his hand on my shoulder encouragingly, and excitement fizzled through my core. I wanted his hand there, strong, comforting. But I bashfully shrugged it off, uncomfortable with my parents being so close.

"And yet..." said my mom, "...she still manages to be single. How has my daughter reached the age of thirty and not yet found herself engaged, I wonder?"

"Oh my Lord," I said and hid my face in shame. "How many of those have you had?" I whispered, pointing at the champagne glass in my mother's hand.

My father was about to answer that for her when I felt someone tug on my sleeve. I turned around. It was Wesley.

"Oh, hi, Wes," I said. "Isn't this great? This is my mom, Megan. And this is Andrew, my dad."

"Hi!" said Wes. "Um, Zoe, can I talk to you for a second?"

"Why don't you join us?" I said. "Wes is new in town," I explained to my parents. "Giulia and I have taken him in!"

"Um, it kind of needs to be...private," replied Wes.

Okay. That sounded kind of strange, but I wasn't going to say no and make a big deal of it in front of my mom and dad. Or Adrian, who was looking at me with daggers in his eyes.

"Sure thing!" I said and followed Wes away from the crowd.

We passed down a narrow corridor and out into the garden. It was a beautiful, lush place with tropical plants and flowers. Cañon City was incredibly mild in the Winter, and I wasn't surprised that the gardeners had taken full advantage of that. The garden was amazing. At one end was a long pond bordered by polished stone slabs. A set of lamps hung over it, below which I could see the enormous, wide backs of koi carp swimming beneath. It was beautiful.

"What is it, Wes?" I said. "What do you want to talk about?"

"Listen, Zoe," he said. "I've been wanting to ask this for a while."

"Ask me what?" I replied. The way he was speaking made me nervous. Too nervous.

"Zoe, I...I want to take you out. Like, on a date. I really like you. I think you're pretty—really pretty and nice, and I want to show you how much I...I like you," Wes said. He stumbled over his own words and delivered the entire speech to me while looking at the floor.

"Oh, Wes," I said. "That's really sweet of you, it is."

"So...so you'll go with me?" he said eagerly.

I sighed. "Wes, I'd...like to, but I can't."

Wesley stopped pouting and took a step away. "What do you mean?" he said incredulously. "You can't? Why...why not?"

"Wes," I said. "I think you're great. And you'll meet someone here, I know it. Giulia will help you. She has plenty of friends. But I just don't feel the same way."

"But, how can you not...feel the same way?" said Wes. It was like his brain had short-circuited. I felt pity for him, but at the same time, I felt anxious to be alone with him out here. He was still almost a stranger to me, someone I hardly knew.

"I'm going to go back inside now," I said. "But let me know how you're doing later, okay?"

I turned and walked inside. Then I heard Wes splutter.

"But...but...you *can't*! I won't let you go!"

I turned around.

"Wesley," I said politely but firmly. "I mean this. I'm not going on a date with you. You need to accept that and move on. Okay? Otherwise, we'll both get hurt. We're still friends, okay? Don't do anything to spoil that, Wesley. Please?"

He didn't say anything, just stared sulkily out at the garden as I left. I thought I heard him mutter, but I didn't pay it any attention. I couldn't go on a date with Wesley; I just couldn't. I could look past his shyness and awkwardness. I even thought he was attractive. But there was something I could no longer deny to myself.

I wanted someone else.

I was almost at the front door when I saw Adrian standing there. He saw me coming too late and turned to walk back down the corridor.

*

"*Cara Zoe*," said Giulia when she found me sitting by myself, halfway down a vodka tonic. "What's wrong, beautiful girl? Tonight's a night for fun and ce-le-*bra*-tion!" she said, swaying her hips over to where I was sitting on a stone bench in the greenhouse. The party was really going now. Adrian had placed a DJ in the main hall, and people were spilling out and into the garden where Wes and I had met earlier.

Giulia made me laugh with her goofy dance moves, but the truth was, my head was spinning. I couldn't get over how fast things were changing. I'd known Adrian felt some way about me, but this was too much. And I couldn't exactly tell his sister that I'd seen him spying on me, could I? After all, if I did, it would bring her one step closer to finding out about what happened at the funeral. And I couldn't let that happen. What had happened with Wes was just an awkward situation, and we'd find time to talk about it soon enough, but I was so confused.

The thought of a nice guy like Wesley asking me on a date should have made me overjoyed. After all, hadn't I spent the whole summer wishing someone would?

And now someone had, and I'd turned him down.

All because I was hung up on Adrian, a billionaire doctor at my hospital, the guy who'd always looked down on me and couldn't *possibly* be interested in me.

Except now I'd caught him spying on me. I knew he was checking on me and Wes, just looking out for me. But was there more to it than that? It was like Adrian had been protecting me all my life. From that incident with the boy who teased me, showing up with flowers and chocolates (no doubt at Adrian's command).

There was another night when he came home after graduating from medical school. I'd just begun working full-time as a nurse, and Giulia had dragged us out to some nightclub. It was fun, but the whole time we were there, Adrian had just sat at the bar watching me and Giulia enjoying ourselves.

I was beginning to get the feeling by then that Adrian didn't like me. Maybe he thought I was butting in on time he could have spent with his sister. Maybe he didn't like the idea of us going to nightclubs, places Adrian thought were a waste of time.

But something had happened that night that I'd been confused about. While Giulia and I danced together, a guy butted in, annoying us by trying to dance with me. He'd gotten in the way. I was enjoying the attention in a kind of passive way when suddenly, he'd put his hands around my waist.

It was gross, and I wouldn't say I liked it, but as I stepped away, the guy leaned in, leering at me. *"Come on, sweetheart,"* he crooned in a brash, drunken sort of way. *"Don't you wanna dance?"*

Then, suddenly, Adrian was there. He'd crossed the dancefloor quicker than I thought possible and stood between us. He didn't say anything, and I could see his broad shoulders were tense and squared against the creep, who sauntered off. We didn't see any more of him that evening.

"Hey," I said, and he spun around, the fire still in his eyes. I leaned towards him to make myself heard. *"Thanks. That guy was a creepy jerk. I owe you one."*

I looked at him in the lights, and as I did, my waist brushed against his thigh. I thought I felt something taut, strong within him. Like he was...

Like he was hard?

Adrian glowered at me, and I assumed I'd pissed him off by getting myself into an uncomfortable situation. *"It was nothing,"* he growled and wandered off. It made me feel stupid, and I shrugged the thought of him off. But now, that memory returned to me in a different light.

Could Adrian Lawson really like me? Was it possible that what happened at his mother's funeral wasn't just a one-time thing?

Was it possible he still wanted me?

"It's just like you always say, Giulia," I sighed. "*Men.*"

Chapter 6

Adrian

I felt guilty all the next day. The party had gone well—it was a nice way to reintroduce myself to the community, and though I hadn't lived permanently in Cañon City since before I went to college, I was surprised how many people remembered me from the old days. Not too surprised, though. I guess I'd become pretty notorious in recent years.

One thing kept nagging away at me, though, and that was Zoe.

She'd seen me.

I knew it was wrong to spy on her, but I did it anyway. Why?

Well, firstly, because I didn't trust Wesley. He seemed nice enough, but I knew from the moment I first saw him that there was something I didn't like about him. And while I didn't have any evidence, I didn't feel as though it was an accident that Giulia had left her keys at home the day my car was vandalized. And, more to the point, I wouldn't say I liked how he followed Zoe around.

I'd always been protective of Glitter Girl in high school. While

I sat in my office that evening catching up on my emails, I remembered the incident with Mike Brenshaw. The day after he humiliated Zoe at school, I followed him home and confronted him at his front door.

"You're gonna make it up to her," I said, holding him by his shirt cuffs on the porch of his house. *"Or we're gonna have a big problem."*

Okay, so I was sixteen at the time; hormones were running wild and out of control. Whatever. But something in me thought of Zoe as being like family. *Cara Zoe*, like my mom used to say before she died. I wanted nothing more than to make sure she was safe, even if I hated her and she was annoying.

While I sat brooding over the events at the party, Wesley's silly declaration of love, and her less-than-enthusiastic response, I heard my cellphone ringing. It was Megan Hollis.

"Megan?" I said. "How are you? What can I do to help?"

"You're not going to like this, Adrian," she said.

I froze. Had Zoe said something? Done something?

"What is it?" I said nervously.

"Dr. Frisk is sick," she said.

"Is he okay? The guy's not getting any younger."

"Oh, he's going to be fine. He's up and about, but if anything happens tonight on cardio or in the trauma unit, he's going to be a serious risk to patients. I need someone to be on-call tonight."

"Let me guess," I said. "Matthews and Connor are on vacation."

"You got it," said Megan in a sing-song voice. She was remarkably cheerful for a woman sentencing me to eight hours in a cramped, uncomfortable dorm room on the opposite side of the hospital parkway.

"Okay, Megan," I said. "But I'm claiming overtime." She

laughed. We both knew I was going to do no such thing.

"I really appreciate that, Adrian. You know, Zoe's still around. Just spoke to her. Why don't the two of you get coffee? Bye for now!"

"I'll see you when I see you, Megan." I put the phone down. *Crap.*

*

I knew she'd find me eventually. And find me she did. Zoe discovered me at 7 pm, spooning the foul, black instant coffee in the breakroom into a stained, polystyrene cup. Not my finest hour.

"Why are you drinking that sludge?" she said curiously.

"I can't stand the coffee machine," I said. "It's too weak. I'm Italian, Zoe. My mom gave me an espresso every day when I was in junior high."

There was silence between us for a moment. I could practically hear her thinking about me, studying me. Was she mad? I couldn't tell.

"You know..." she said, "...if you really hate the coffee machine so much, why don't you use the HAL 9000?"

"The what?" I said.

"You know about the HAL 9000, don't you?" Zoe repeated. I had no idea what she was talking about.

"You're gonna have to speak English, Zoe," I said.

"It's named after the robot! In the movie!" she said.

"Oh," I said. "I didn't know there was a coffee machine."

"Wow," laughed Zoe. "You know, maybe if you were a little bit nicer, someone would have told you about it by now!"

"I can't help being a grump," I said as I followed her down the corridor. "It's the way I am."

As I watched Zoe lead the way down the corridor, my eyes followed the line of her shoulders. It was the end of the day now, most of the staff had gone home, and the night shift was starting. I'd be able to sleep it out if I wanted—the chances of being called in to perform surgery were minimal at Cañon City—but I knew I wouldn't be able to sleep. I was planning on getting some work done on an article for the AMA journal.

Eventually, we arrived at a small kitchen somewhere in the knotted, tangled mess of corridors between the cardiology and gynecology departments.

"Technically, this is gynae property, but I'll have you know, Dr. Frisk and I were investors," she said. Sitting on the countertop was a gorgeous espresso machine. Zoe popped a pod for me and pressed the button. The smell was intoxicating.

She handed the cup to me, and I took a swig. "That's the stuff," I said. "Damn."

"Frisk isn't feeling well, so I'm on call tonight," I explained.

"And you're drinking coffee?" said Zoe. "You don't sleep much, do you?"

"What about you?" I said, leaning against the wall while she made herself a long black. "Why are *you* here?"

"I don't know," she said. "I should have gone home an hour ago. Guess I lost track of time."

"Well, it's time to go. You're in again tomorrow, right?"

She shook her head. "I've got the day off. Well, hope you enjoy your coffee!"

I nodded, holding out my cup in a gesture of appreciation. But Zoe didn't leave.

"I've never seen an on-call room," she said. "Can you show me?"

*

I unlocked the door and held it open, flicking on the light. There wasn't much in there. A sink, obviously. A kettle and a fridge for keeping snacks. The wall was decorated with Dr. Frisk's memorabilia, flyers, health cards, and hand-me-down posters from bygone eras of medicine. Some junior residents with a particularly wicked sense of humor had tacked up a poster from the 1950s with a doctor who endorsed smoking. "DOCTOR DRISCOLL RECOMMENDS ONE PACK A DAY OF COOL MILDS FOR CLEARING CONGESTION AND SOOTHING THE THROAT!" I thought back to Eleanor May, who hadn't touched a cigarette in two weeks and was finally starting to feel her old self again. *That* was progress.

"Damn, it's so poky and depressing," said Zoe. "Kind of suits you."

"Oh, what?" I said, exasperatedly, putting down my cup of coffee on the sideboard. "Moody grump of a man deserves a miserable little room to sleep in?"

Zoe nodded cheerily and smiled a big toothy grin at me. She was cute. I couldn't deny it. "If the shoe fits," she said.

"Well, I wasn't actually planning on sleeping much in here. I was going to be working in my office."

"And now here you are, goofing off with me instead. Looks like

Billionaire Doctor Adrian Lawson isn't so perfect as he thought," said Zoe.

"You're full of crap," I said. "Besides, only one of us is trying to be perfect, and it's Glitter Girl, not me."

"At least I'm not spying on other people's private conversations," said Zoe. "Hey, do you have any hidden microphones or cameras in your fancy new place? So you can, like, watch the girls in the bathroom and stuff?"

I rolled my eyes. "You're so dumb," I said. "I didn't mean to spy. I just wanted—"

"To be overprotective and weird, like you normally are. You and Wes have a lot in common, you know."

"Oh, cut it out, Zoe," I said. The coffee was hitting my system, but I was still irritated and tired. "I'm not in the mood for this right now."

"Oh yeah?" she said. "Too bad. Because you don't just get to creep around behind my back and not have to explain yourself, Adrian. Not given our history."

"We don't have a history," I retorted.

"What do we have then?" she said defiantly. Zoe was practically squaring up to me now. There wasn't much space between us in the tiny on-call room. I could smell the scent of her hair and skin lotion, a soft smell.

"You're just jealous..." I said, "...that Wes is asking you out and not me."

"I do wonder why you're so interested in me..." she said bitterly, "...if you think I'm so annoying."

"And I wonder why you're so mean to me..." I snapped, "...when everyone thinks you're the nicest girl in town!"

We stopped for a moment. We were standing so close to each other now.

And then, just like that, Zoe dived into my arms.

Our lips met, and we kissed while my hands found their way about her waist. The material of her nurse's uniform was so thin I could feel her body through it, touch her waist, her hips, and it inflamed my desire, made me want more. I was hard now and realized, almost off-hand, that I'd been hard for her for a while, maybe since before we got into this room. This room was tiny but isolated, private, with a bed. For us.

"What are we—" Zoe said, but she didn't have time to finish her sentence because I was pulling her hair gently away from her scalp where strands of her ponytail had come loose and lie around her shoulders. I was kissing her neck, and her words turned to babble and were replaced with soft moans which spoke to her desperate need for me.

There was nothing either of us could say that could justify or stop this. I didn't have time. In a heartbeat, I'd lifted Zoe's top and pulled it from her head, and she stood in front of me, defiant and proud, the lightly tanned skin around her waist calling to me. I lost any sense of gentlemanly etiquette and tipped her onto the bed, where she sat, shocked and mute, looking up at me with eyes that seemed to show nothing but excitement and anticipation.

I bent down, and now my mouth found its way down beyond her neck, to her chest, where I kissed her hard, letting my teeth sit gently on her skin for a moment. She gasped with excitement, and I lifted my head, looking with pride at the livid little bruise I'd left there.

"You're delicate," I whispered, tipping her onto her back, where she lay while I removed her trousers and panties.

I kneeled and unbuttoned my shirt for her while she rested her head on a pillow and stared at me with fascination. Her hand reached out and grasped mine, and I took it happily while I set to work. After planting a few kisses on the inside of her thigh, Zoe shuddered as I pressed my tongue to the hot, wet warmth between her legs. I delighted in the thought that my tongue was still a little hot from the coffee as she yelped and shuddered with pleasure. I slowed down a little, letting her dictate the rhythm, matching the pace at which I licked her pussy with the slow, undulating rolling of her hips. "That's it," I whispered between mouthfuls. "That's my girl."

But I felt her tugging at my shoulder with a free hand before I could complete the act, and I looked deep into Zoe Hollis' eyes. For the first time, I saw her smile and really appreciated it. I felt delight coursing through me to be the only one who could see her smile and know that she was smiling in appreciation of how much she enjoyed my mouth on her. But her eyes spoke of a different need.

"Fuck me, Adrian," she said. "Please. I need it."

I nodded and wiped my mouth. I climbed up onto the little bed beside her. Our bodies pressed together in the cramped space as her hand undid my trousers and began to work them off. They were barely free of my ankles when I felt Zoe's hand take hold of my cock, reaching under my boxer shorts to touch its length and width. "In me..." she said, "...please, please."

I slipped a hand between her legs as I kneeled up above her to check that she was ready. My finger slipped inside with ease, and she gave a little laugh. I knew now that Zoe Hollis had never been so wet in her life as she was for me at this moment, and I dove inside her, happily abandoning myself to the carnage of our sweaty, hurried, hot union.

I wasted no time and knew I couldn't savor her now like I'd done that fateful summer one year ago. I fucked her, pinning her beneath me so I could more easily kiss her face, her mouth, and whisper to her how good she felt, how tight and warm but oh so easy to take until I felt her shuddering, felt her muscles clench and release all at once as the slow, deep cries that echoed up from inside her turned into shouts of satisfaction.

I came for her, pulsing inside as hot jets of my semen dripped slowly from her cunt and into the sheets of the bed, and gripped her with tears in my eyes at the sweet feeling of her before rolling off her and gathering her shaking, supple body in my arms.

When I woke an hour later to my phone buzzing, it was dark, and she was gone.

Chapter 7

Zoe

What have I done?

To give myself to Adrian like that, freely, enthusiastically. To have said the things I'd said.

It would have been so easy to be angry with him. We'd had sex on hospital grounds. I could lose my job if anyone found out. Both our reputations would be tarnished.

There was no way anyone could find out. Doctors and nurses frequented the on-call suites often. Though not usually for bouts of amazing, mind-blowingly good sex that resulted in powerful orgasms.

I guess that was mine and Adrian's thing.

After I got home that night, I showered and got into bed. I didn't have the heart to wake Adrian. I knew I'd want to talk about it and imagined that was the last thing he wanted. It was all so confusing.

Sleep came at some point, and the next day I woke, I checked my clock and realized it was 10 am. I couldn't believe I'd slept so well or peacefully. I guiltily thought that it was probably the incredible night I'd had with Adrian.

Giulia!

Guilt threatened to consume me whole before I got up and made coffee and scrambled some eggs. Outside, it was already getting warm, and in a spirit of unabashed body confidence, I decided to put on some incredibly cute pink shorts that Giulia had given me for my birthday. They weren't exactly my color, but I liked the look once I'd paired them up with a sky-blue shirt. *Blue-sky thinking.* That was the way forward.

I tidied the house and took out my trash. As I got to the bin, I looked over and saw Wes.

He was soaping his car, a black Hyundai. I saw him toss the sponge in the bucket and go to get his hose. He looked different, somehow. Confident. More imposing.

He turned around, and our eyes met. His dark eyes. They made me shudder. The likeness was uncanny. But even though he seemed to look a little bit like Adrian, certain things just couldn't be like the man I knew. Wes had dark circles under his eyes, for one. And his face wasn't as handsome, lacking Adrian's strong features.

"Morning," said Wes, and he continued to wash his car.

"How are you doing?" I asked, trying to be nice. Even if I'd had to be firm with Wesley about his feelings, I didn't want Wes to feel awkward around me.

"Just fine," he said. His voice sounded strange. It was like he was more confident. Stern, even. He didn't hesitate or pause or whisper.

"All right," I said. "See you soon."

I went back inside and locked the front door.

I had a new fantasy novel that I had been itching to start for weeks. The book was good enough to make me forget about what Adrian and I had done yesterday. I was nearly halfway when Giulia dropped by midday.

"You..." she said as soon as I opened the door, "...have not eaten lunch."

"Do you have psychic powers?" I said, placing one hand on my hip and another on the doorframe.

"That's right!" she said, grinning. "I knew just from looking at your palms. Behold!"

She reached out and flipped over my hands, one by one, then lifted up her right hand. In it was a hamper.

"You know what time it is," she said.

I sighed. "It's picnic time!"

*

We drove out for a while into Rouse Park. Once we'd parked, we found the trail that led by the Arkansas River. It was pretty quiet for a Sunday, and eventually, when we managed to find the right spot, Giulia laid down a blanket and started to unpack. "Where do you get all this stuff?"

"It's the secret of my people," replied Giulia, and we both laughed.

Giulia was supermodel-skinny, but she ate like an Italian. Fresh bread, cheese, fruit...I was amazed. "Mama used to say she hated American sandwiches," Giulia said. "But I've got baloney, in case you feel the need."

I did. We snacked for a while, hanging out in the sun. Once

we'd finished eating, we lay on the blanket, looking up above the trees that ran by the river. Giulia was almost half-asleep when I told her about Wes at the party.

"He said what?" she cried, sitting up. "Oh no. You don't like him, do you?"

"Not like that," I said. "It would honestly be so much easier if he wasn't being weird about it."

"Is he being weird?" said Giulia. "He seems pretty normal to me."

"I'm happy you think so," I said, and we both chuckled.

"Seriously, though, *cara*, if he's being a dummy, you just tell Adrian. The guy adores you. He'll go have a word with him."

I shifted uneasily and sat up too. "Adrian doesn't adore me," I said. I checked my watch. It was 3 pm. He'd be getting off work soon. Poor Adrian. He'd hardly had time to sleep a wink this weekend.

"Don't feel sorry for him," said Giulia when I mentioned it to her. "He loves being a doctor. It's all he ever wanted to do. I swear, if it weren't for the fast cars and fancy beach houses, he'd give all that money away. Don't tell him I told you this..." Giulia said conspiratorially, "...but Adrian's, like, super-sensitive. He wants to help people. That's what he's always wanted to do."

"Really?" I said. "But at school, he was so..."

Giulia looked at me. "Wild?" she said.

"Yeah!" I replied.

"I think it was hard for him," said Giulia. "Adrian was always asking questions about home, and Dad. He wanted to know more, but Mom wouldn't budge. She just used to smile and close her eyes and say, 'What is closed, holds the secret.'"

"What does that mean?" I asked. "Is that some kind of Italian saying?"

"I don't know." Giulia looked thoughtful and stared hard into the trees. "It certainly means *something.*"

"What does?" said a voice behind us. I jumped up.

"Adrian!" said Giulia, standing up. "How did you find us?"

Adrian took out his cell phone and held it up. "A little thing called Find My Phone..." he said. "You really should turn it off, or I'm going to be out looking for my baby sister."

They embraced, and then he turned to look at me. "How are you, Zoe?" he said politely.

"I'm...good," I said. I didn't know where to look. I hadn't expected to see Adrian less than a day after we'd had sex at the hospital. I felt my left leg trembling slightly just thinking about it.

"What's up with you guys?" said Giulia petulantly. "Why so serious all the time? Why are you always fighting?"

"We're not fighting," said Adrian, glancing at me. *Are we?* Then, he smiled—a real smile. I didn't know what he was thinking, but he looked warm and genuine, and for a moment, I felt a sense of peace rushing through me, through the valley and the grass beneath my bare feet.

"Sure," I said and felt my body burn for him again.

We passed the afternoon in casual conversation, but it didn't get lost on me how Adrian was staring at me. I caught him a few times, and he only looked away when Giulia would spring up from her position. My stomach was tight with nerves...both nervous excitement and guilt for not telling Giulia what happened. At this point, it would hurt more if I lost her over something I wasn't sure was happening.

When the sun had completely set, we packed up. Giulia had to meet some of her colleagues from the school for drinks in town, and Adrian offered to give me a lift. I wasn't entirely comfortable, and thought Giulia would see through his offer. But Giulia seemed fine about it.

"She has no idea, does she?" I said, once we were in the car and Giulia had driven off.

"Why would she?" he replied.

"It's not right...What we're doing."

"Are you worried we've made a mistake?" he said. We turned a corner, and the stores and road signs started to crop up along the road into Cañon City.

"Are you?" I countered.

Adrian took a deep breath but kept his eyes on the road. Then he started to speak, low and slow, and I found myself lost in his voice.

"The first time, I didn't know what I wanted," he started. "I was scared. I'd lost my mother, and I was worried for Giulia. I was in awe of you. You were so good with her through that time, Zoe. I'm grateful, I really am." But then his face clouded over.

"It wasn't fair of me to ask you for what I asked," he said. "I know you've always known how you felt about me. Or at least, when we were younger, I knew you had a thing for me. But I didn't know how I felt about you until that day. And it wasn't the right way to show it."

"But this time..." he continued, "...last night."

There was a pause.

"That didn't seem like a mistake," he said. "I liked it too much. I wanted it too much. I knew what I wanted from you, and you knew what you wanted from me. Wouldn't it be fair to say we got what we wanted?"

I took a moment to think. "I liked it. I wanted it. But I don't know where we go from here. I don't know what to do next."

He nodded. "Can we both think about what we want..." he said, "...and then talk?"

"Yeah. Sounds good." Somehow, we'd arrived at my house. I guess we'd been talking so slowly, thinking about what we would say.

Adrian surprised me when he reached for my hand and gently placed a kiss on it, deep brown eyes twinkling under the dim light from the light pole outside. Air caught in my throat, and when he released his hold, my hand froze in place, wanting to remain connected.

"I'll catch you tomorrow on the ward," he said after a beat. "And, Zoe?"

I looked at him, my unkissed hand on the passenger door. "Yeah?"

"Take care."

I got out, and as I saw him drive away, up the hill to his house, I smiled. But it wasn't my usual smile. I always smile at everyone I meet. I greet the day with a smile. But that smile is big, wide, and meant to say; *It's okay, I'll do what I can to make you smile too.* This smile wasn't like that. It was small, personal, and private. This smile was just for me.

Chapter 8

Adrian

The night after I drove Zoe home, I slept dreamlessly and deeply. I woke up Monday morning and put my hand on the pendant around my neck.

The pendant was small and made of gold. It was heavy, too, probably solid all the way through. A flat disc, maybe made out of a coin or something. I didn't know. But my mom gave it to me when I was fifteen and told me to keep it safe. I wore it, usually beneath my shirt. I guess it was just my way of keeping her close to me. I always liked to hold and look at the pendant when I was thinking things over. In this case, it was Zoe Hollis who was occupying my thoughts. I was on-call again that night, covering for Frisk, and I was sure I'd run into Zoe at some point. I needed to have a strategy to avoid things getting—well, out of control, this time.

I got up and decided to go for a run to clear my head. There was a way out through the grand backyard of my new house into the fields beyond that led down to the nature trail. I jogged on and was just starting to break into a sweat when my phone began to ring from where I'd placed it inside the zip-up pocket of my running shorts.

I stopped and grumbled a little to myself while I took it out. I saw that it was Charlie, my fund manager, calling. I answered the phone.

"Charlie? What's up?"

"Adrian? Is that you? You sound out of breath, buddy. What have you been up to, superstar?"

I scowled, happy that Charlie couldn't see me. I hated it when he called me buddy. It usually meant he had some bad news to break to me.

"I'm just fine, champ. I was out for a jog when you called me up."

"That's the spirit. Get a bit of exercise! Clears the head, sharpens the mind—"

"Cut to the chase, Charlie," I said dryly. Obviously, he had something bad to tell me.

"Well, everything's going well with the fund, as you know. In fact, I've had Chris draw up some interesting investments in the Midwest for you that might be promising. Solar, wind energy, et cetera..."

I was heavily invested in renewable energies and technology, as well as more traditional and stable prospects like natural resources, minerals, and so on. I had a good spread of interests across my portfolio, and, at this point, I was able to live well on my returns.

"Sounds good, Charlie. But that's not what you wanted to talk to me about today, is it?"

He cursed. "You're good, Lawson. I'll give you that. Yeah, we do have a small issue."

"Go on."

"On Friday, someone filed fifteen separate complaints concerning your asset management, investment practices, and taxes. I'm talking *serious* accusations of mismanagement and insider trading. Someone's accused you of setting up a boiler room in partnership with that energy firm, Liederman and Co., you know the one, right?"

"What? That's crazy. Do the accusations have any kind of weight?"

"This isn't 1985, Adrian. They're bound to be investigated. And it could put a stop to our business for a while. Especially if the IRS decides to audit us."

"The IRS? Why would they get involved?"

"Whoever's made the complaints, they've gone to everyone. FINRA, the SEC, IRS. The works. I don't know what to tell you, Adrian. We run a tight ship and a clean business up here; you know that. Hell, you set this place up yourself. All we can do is get our business materials together."

I thought about my vandalized Maserati, currently sitting in a workshop in Modena.

"No, here's what you're going to do, Charlie. I want you to launch counter-complaints and appeals. This is obviously harassment. These accusations don't have any basis in reality. I'd like you to get together an overview of our tax contributions, portfolio structure, and disclosed affiliations and send them to the relevant parties. We're going to come right back at whoever's doing this."

"Adrian, that's a pretty big commitment. And besides, we don't even know who's doing this—"

"You don't go on the defensive when someone is trying to

disrupt your business. The best form of defense is attack. You know that, Charlie. Now, file the counter-allegations, and see what comes of it."

There was a brief pause before I heard Charlie buzz his assistant.

"Cancel my appointments for the rest of the day, please, Susan," he said before hanging up.

*

That night, at 2 am, I woke to the sound of my pager beeping. I switched on the light.

It took me ten minutes to get dressed and get into the hospital from the on-call room. By the time I was there, they were prepping Mr. McCabe for surgery.

"Patient was admitted following complaints of arrhythmia and shortness of breath. After admission, he was secured in the ward. At about 1:50 am, he went into heart failure," explained Greg as we washed our hands and got changed into scrubs.

I looked at the charts. It didn't look good.

There was only one option.

"I've got a plan. Mask up," I said. "We're out of time."

We were finished in two hours. At 4:15 am, I closed the incision. By 4:30 am, we were out. Greg looked exhausted and pale.

"You did great," I said. "You kept your cool. That's important. The next time you'll know what to do and how to do the procedure."

He looked at me but didn't smile. "I was useless," he said, looking at his feet. "He would have died if you hadn't been here."

I looked at him. I'm not the most cheerful person, but my stoic view of the world makes for a good life lesson.

"People will die," I said. "And sometimes, you'll have done everything right, and they'll still die. We can't always prevent it. Mr. McCabe's certainly going to need a pacemaker implanted if he wants any kind of a healthy life, and someone else will do that surgery and live with its consequences. That's what doctors do."

I could see Greg wasn't in the mood. I sent him home an hour early before his shift was over. The chances of another emergency that night were pretty slim. But I couldn't sleep. Adrenalin was still coursing through my veins, keeping me alert and awake. I decided to 'call it morning', as doctors and nurses like to say. And luckily, I knew just where to get the perfect cup of coffee.

McCabe had been moved to intensive care by the time I got back to the cardiology department. He'd be back on the ward in a few days. Zoe was sitting at the front desk of the hospital.

"I brought you a coffee," I said. She looked up at me with dark circles under her eyes and smiled. I leaned against the desk and looked down at her, that soft, blonde hair and the nape of her neck.

It was strange to think of partying at a time like that, but seeing Zoe's hair sent me a memory from long ago before everything had gotten so complicated.

It was after I'd graduated from medical school. I came back to Cañon City for a few days. By then, Zoe had just begun working as a nurse at the hospital, and we had a lot more to talk about as medical practitioners. Giulia had insisted we go celebrate, which of course, meant a trip to the nightclub. I wasn't really feeling up for it (I've never exactly been the partying type), but I went anyway to spend time with my sister.

In the darkness of the club, I sat sulkily by the bar with a beer in my hand, watching Zoe and Giulia dance. As I saw them spin, the colored lights of the club caught on the back of Zoe's neck, and I instantly felt a throbbing sensation in my pants. As I turned back to the bar, confused and more than a little ashamed of myself, I met the eyes of an attractive blonde woman there at the bar.

"Well, handsome," she said, grinning. *"I guess I know who's buying me my next drink."*

I'd met plenty of women like this before, and normally I would have taken her up on the offer. But I couldn't get Zoe out of my head that night. It was crazy and dumb. After all, I'd barely seen her since I left high school. She was Giulia's best friend (and like a second daughter to my mother). Why did I feel the way I felt about her that night?

"Sorry..." I said, *"...not tonight."* The blonde girl pursed her lips and turned away, no doubt seeking someone else's attention. I told myself I'd turned her down because I was out with my sister, and it would have been inappropriate to run off with some stranger.

But the truth was, I only had eyes for Zoe Hollis that night.

I tried to resist, but I couldn't help myself. I turned back and looked for her.

Then, I saw a guy.

He'd sauntered up behind Zoe and Giulia and was dancing with them now. I bristled with annoyance but stayed myself. I didn't want to look like some psycho.

But when I saw him reach out and put a hand across Zoe's waist while he swayed his hips towards her like a jerk, I couldn't help myself.

I marched over, through the mass of pulsing bodies, and stepped between them. The guy looked at me, confused, and I glared at him. He muttered something and shot me an ugly look before wandering off into the crowd.

"Hey," said Zoe, and I turned around. I was expecting a lecture. But I didn't get one.

Instead, she leaned in close and said in my ear, over the dance music, *"Thanks. That guy was a creepy jerk. I owe you one."*

As she said it, I shook my head, and felt her body move against mine on the crowded dancefloor. She put a hand on my arm, and squeezed it affectionately, and I felt my heart pound like it wanted to jump out of my chest. Her waist brushed against my thigh, almost touching the hard-on I was concealing in my pants...

I didn't know what to say.

I shrugged. *"It was nothing,"* I growled, and stalked off.

Back in the cardiology department, I slumped in a chair. I was bent over, my head blistering with pain. It was like all the focus and adrenaline had drained out of me.

We sat there in silence for a little while before Zoe said, "You're amazing."

I looked at her to see if it was a joke. But it wasn't. Zoe was practically beaming at me. Considering she was the happiest person I knew, I'd never seen her so overjoyed.

"Clarissa told me what happened in there. She says she's never seen anyone look so calm in surgery before."

"Believe me, I wasn't that calm." I wasn't lying. Such a delicate procedure was not my idea of a quiet night while on call.

"You seem it. And he's alive and well. Thanks to you."

I looked at her. "Guess I'm not such a bad guy as you think."

She laughed. "Adrian, I never thought you were a bad guy. I've thought a lot of things about you, but never that."

"Oh yeah? What kind of things?"

Zoe smirked and looked down at the chart she was filling in.

"Have you ever thought that you might want to go on a date with me?"

The words just came out. I hardly meant them to, but they did. I couldn't help but ask her.

She looked up at me again. "You really mean that?"

"Of course I mean it," I said. "I'm crazy about you. Isn't it obvious?"

We both smiled at one another. We couldn't own up to the amazing night we'd spent in the on-call room on Saturday. But both of us were thinking about it.

"Okay," she said. "I've got the day off tomorrow. Why don't you take me out?"

"It's a deal," I said.

"What are we going to tell Giulia?" said Zoe. "She's going to find out eventually."

"As long as we're happy, I think she'll be overjoyed. Her best friend and her brother dating—it isn't exactly going to make us spend less time with her, is it?"

"I guess not." Zoe gazed out of the window. "Sun's coming up."

We watched as rosy, golden beams began to push through the slats of the Venetian blinds by the wall and thought about what the future would bring.

Chapter 9

Zoe

I'd played it cool, but I was practically in hysterics after Adrian left. *A date?* A real date, just the two of us together, bonding and enjoying each other's company. I was thrilled at the idea. I'd been impressed by him and how open he was about his feelings for me. It felt as though we'd turned a corner. And I was happy that we wouldn't be sneaking around, uncertain about how the other felt from now on. Amazing as sex with him was, it had left me emotionally drained and uncertain about what he thought of me.

I was so excited that I could hardly sleep when I got home that morning. But at 4 pm that afternoon, I got up, showered, and made myself a coffee. I wasn't sure whether to eat anything. Was Adrian going to take me for dinner? He'd been pretty cagey and mysterious about his plans, but I knew he'd plan something interesting and special for us.

I got dressed in a cute outfit and worked hard to search my wardrobe for something that *wasn't* yellow. Eventually, I found the perfect outfit. It was a sea-green, ruched dress with one shoulder—perfect for going to a date or the movies and comfortable enough to move in if we wanted to take a walk. I slipped on a pair of Mary Janes that would look equally stylish in a restaurant or on the dusty streets of Cañon City.

"Zoe, you've done it again," I said to myself, looking in the mirror. "Estella would be proud."

I called an Uber to take me up to Adrian's. We'd agreed I'd leave from there since we might get caught if Giulia saw us leaving together. It felt exciting and fun heading to my secret rendezvous as the sun lowered gently over the horizon. But at the same time, I couldn't pretend that I wasn't doing something wrong.

Should I tell Giulia? Maybe I could make up some kind of excuse. Tell her that Adrian and I had agreed to get coffee. I took out my phone.

Then, I put it away. I didn't know how to lie to Giulia like that, and I didn't want to start now. The best I could do was a sin of omission.

I wasn't sure what to say if she asked me where I'd been, though.

I waited until the Uber was right outside my door before dashing to it, closing the door quickly and praying Giulia was busy in the back somewhere. My heart rate slowed down the further we were from my street.

As we climbed the hill out of Cañon City, I saw the shadows of Adrian's enormous mansion looming over the skyline. It felt like I was being carried to the mysterious lair of some shadowy figure, like in a storybook. But at the same time, despite my feelings of apprehension, I only felt glad at the thought of seeing him like this.

At the gate, I got out and thanked the driver. I turned back to watch the Uber descend the hill and looked up at the enormous, dark gate and the tower of the old house in the sunlight. Despite the warm weather and the light cascading over the scene, I trembled a little. Not from cold. From something else, a feeling whose edges I couldn't quite grasp within myself.

I buzzed the doorbell, but there was no answer.

I buzzed again. Still nothing.

Had he forgotten about me? Warmth flooded my cheeks. Was Adrian about to stand me up?

But then, the gate slowly swung open. And somewhere off to the side of the house and its driveway, I heard the rev of a car engine.

Slowly, out from under the shadows of the house, a sleek, dark car with a spoiler on its back emerged, growling over the driveway. It moved towards the gate, then stopped.

I watched as Adrian eased himself out of his Chevvy Corvette. I was relieved to see he was wearing a suit with no tie. Obviously, I hadn't overdressed myself. I made my way gingerly over to the car. He strode confidently towards me.

"Is your Maserati not back from the shop yet?" I asked. Flashes of memory from when we found his car in Giulia's garage came to me. Giulia had told me that the detective had yet to make headway on who would have defaced Adrian's car like that and threatened him.

"Still on its way back from Italy," he said apologetically. "I thought the Corvette would do."

"I'm sure it will," I laughed, and he leaned in to embrace me.

We'd never touched like this before—gentle, delicate, as though he wanted to make sure I was comfortable with his arms around me. I felt that lightness in my head that was beginning to accompany Adrian's presence in my life. His touch was warm, and I could smell his cologne, the heady, soft scent of sandalwood making me take a breath. Something about his presence overwhelmed me in the most incredible way.

"Come on," he said, pulling away from me and taking my hand. "We don't want to be late."

"Late for what?" I said. "Did you make a reservation somewhere?"

He looked mischievous. "Not quite. It's a little bit of a drive, but I'm sure you'll appreciate the scenery."

We got in, and to my amazement, I saw that we weren't going into town but rather West, out into the desert. "Where are we going?" I said. I guess I imagined that he was taking me to some secret billionaires retreat up in the mountains. But Adrian smiled and just changed the subject. We chatted for a while until Adrian turned the conversation to me.

"I guess we've been so busy arguing and avoiding each other that I haven't really got the chance to ask how you are," he said.

"I'm doing great," I said. I meant it. I was always doing great. Wasn't I?

"Oh, come on, Zoe," he said. "Even you must have your down days."

"Well, sure," I said. "But there's so much to be grateful for. I own my own house, have a job I like, and help people get better. My parents are amazing. My dad's health is incredible, and he's turning sixty next year."

"But what's your plan?" said Adrian. He spoke in a way I hardly recognized, gently, with patience. He was listening to me and taking in my answers.

"My plan?" I chirped back. "I don't know. I guess I like it here, but..."

"But what?" said Adrian, leading me through the conversation as we began to climb uphill onto a plateau. Above us, the stars began to glimmer as the light pollution from the city faded, and we passed through a canyon.

"I guess I've always wondered what it would be like to live somewhere else. I remember Estella when she used to talk about Italy."

"She discussed Italy with you?" said Adrian. "Wow."

"What?" I said. "She never talked about it with you?"

He shook his head slowly, and we dropped out of the canyon and onto the plateau. It was an enormous expanse of flat desert, stretching for miles in every direction, bordered by mountains. We must have been pretty close to the New Mexico border. The Corvette was such a fast-moving car, it had taken us sixty or seventy miles out of the city in forty-five minutes, and I hadn't even noticed.

"I don't know why. Maybe it upset her that my dad died there."

"I've never asked this..." I said, "...but, how did he die?"

"Yeah," said Adrian. "All my mom told me was that he died in a car accident. I was three when it happened, and my mom was pregnant with Giulia at the time. I don't remember much of Italy, to tell you the truth. I don't even remember what Dad looked like. Sometimes I want to go back there, but I don't think Mom would have liked it."

"Why not?" I said. "Wouldn't she want you guys to know where you came from?"

"All she said was that we could never go back. All the time, when we were growing up. I don't know...it's like she was afraid of something. I must have really bothered her by asking because one day she gave me this...." Adrian reached inside his open shirt and removed the little gold pendant from where it hung around his chest. "She said it would bring me good luck and that it belonged to my dad. Kind of hard to imagine him wearing it, but I've kept it close for her."

I smiled. "That's amazing, Adrian." I was beginning to see that under the grump I knew, there was a sensitive, sweet man there. Adrian might keep his feelings close, but he had a big heart. That was for sure.

"We're almost there," he said and started to slow down. He gently eased the car off the side of the road and slowed to a stop. Turning the engine off, he jumped out of the car and stepped round to my side, where he opened the door.

Adrian helped me out of the car, and we walked on for a few minutes.

"It's still so warm out here," I said.

He smiled. "It can get pretty cold at night..." he said, "...but we still have a few hours of warmth left. The sun only just went down."

We came to an enormous boulder. Adrian took my hand and led me around. Out in the distance, purple shadows of the mountains, lofty and enormous, rose up. I was reminded of how beautiful Colorado was at night. When I was little, my dad sometimes drove me through the mountains. I hadn't been out here in ages. It was so thoughtful of Adrian to bring me.

"This is incredible," I said.

He smiled. "I'm glad you like it, but we haven't even found our table yet."

"Table?" I said. "Out here?"

"I wanted to take you for dinner..." he said, "...and I thought this would be a little more special."

As we rounded the rock, I saw it. A small table, covered with a red checkered tablecloth, like the kind you might find at an Italian restaurant. There was even a candle in a wine bottle. It was an amazing sight.

"Oh my God," I said. "How did you get all this out here?"

I could hear a generator humming somewhere a few hundred yards away. "The food's being prepared right now," said Adrian, pulling my seat out for me. I sat down. Above me, a thousand stars swirled into the night; the sky tinted shades of blue and purple and red. It was the most amazing thing I'd ever seen.

Adrian sat himself down at the table and produced a bottle of wine from an ice chest that had been left next to his seat. "I remembered Chardonnay has always been your favorite."

I was blushing uncontrollably. "Adrian, this is already the best date I've ever been on. Thank you. I can't tell you how much fun I'm having."

"Good," he said. "If we're going to do this, we should do it properly."

Dinner began with pasta, as I expected it would. But not just any pasta. This was handmade, tossed in an amazing, creamy sauce, and hand-delivered by the chef, who appeared from a short distance away. "I hope the generator isn't too loud, sir," he said. "It's quite difficult to get power out here at this time of night."

"It's incredibly impressive, Arnold," said Adrian. "And this looks delicious. Thank you."

"Handmade mushroom tortellini, served with a sauce of shallots, garlic, white wine, and cream," said Arnold.

I took a bit. "Delicious," I said. "God, this is incredible."

Arnold nodded politely and left. "Is that your private chef at Cañon Lodge?" I asked.

Adrian nodded. "He's a pretty talented guy. He wasn't thrilled when I told him he'd be cooking in the desert tonight. But Arnold's pretty adaptable."

The food was incredible. "Do you eat like this all the time?" I said. "How are you so healthy?"

Adrian laughed. "I don't know. I run and swim a lot. I look after my body. But no, I don't eat like this all the time. Only on special occasions. And this is a special occasion."

After the pasta, I was served an impressively large steak, with bordelaise sauce, French fries, and tender stem broccoli. As we ate our main course, I looked up at the mountains. "It's breathtaking," I said, staring. Then I heard the sound of music.

It was a violin, its notes soft and sweet on the gentle breeze beginning to sweep over the plateau. I looked up above me, where the music was coming from.

"Maurice is an old friend of mine," said Adrian. "I endowed a scholarship at Julliard, and he was the first person to win it. He's the principal violinist at the Colorado Symphony Orchestra in Denver now. He agreed to come play for us."

I looked up, and Maurice sat on top of the boulder. He was dressed in tails and white tie, sitting cross-legged on a blanket up there, playing with confidence and soulful emotion.

I couldn't believe it! Here I was, sitting at a dinner table in the middle of the desert with Adrian being serenaded by the violin! It was magical. I felt a slight chill as dessert arrived, and Adrian produced a fur shawl from a box under his chair.

"You've thought of everything," I said in wonder as he stood up and draped it around my shoulders. I wanted his hands to linger longer on my neck as he adjusted the shawl, but he sat down. "Is this made from real fur?"

"No," he said, seeming a little offended. "I'm not Cruella de Ville." Arnold appeared again out of the darkness with an elegant slice of chocolate tart served with a dollop of crème fraiche.

"Thanks, Arnold," said Adrian. "This has been lovely. Feel free to pack up now."

"Thank you, sir," he said. "Would the young lady like a coffee before I leave?"

"Yes, thank you."

My heart hammered at how perfect this was; I was sure my jaw would be aching tomorrow from how wide I was smiling right now.

After finishing my coffee and dessert, Maurice began to play a waltz.

"Would you like to dance, *cara?*"

I took Adrian's outstretched hand. I was floating at how glorious it felt to be this smitten around Adrian. For the longest time, I had only felt irritation whenever I saw his face. Okay, maybe not all the time. There were moments when I would ogle at him, and my thoughts would go to naughty places before I chastised myself. But never would I have thought things would have developed into this. A date, out in the desert, with grumpy Adrian.

I rested my head on Adrian's shoulder, feeling safe and comfortable with him in a way I'd never known I would. He pulled me into him and gently placed his hand on my waist as we spun in slow, lazy circles, his feet guiding mine as the music slowly drew close.

After a second dance, easy conversation and draining my cup of coffee, Adrian walked me back to the car, arm-in-arm. He opened the door for me, and we got in. After he sat himself in the driver's seat, I reached out to touch his face. He turned to me, and we kissed, slowly and gently, lit by the moon, which hung large and round in the sky before us, up the hills and out beyond.

"Zoe," he said between kisses. "You're always so sweet and friendly. It makes me want to treat you like royalty."

"I am pretty friendly," I said seductively. "You know…" I said, whispering in his ear, "…the back seats of this car look pretty comfortable."

He smiled and held my hand while he planted a gentle kiss on my cheek. "I think we should take it a little more slowly than we have in the past," he said. I was a little disappointed he didn't want to ravage me again, but I could tell Adrian was doing his best to really give things a chance between us. I appreciated that.

It was more than I'd gotten in the past.

I just hope we hadn't gotten ahead of ourselves and that he was right. That Giulia would be happy for us. I hated to think what would happen if he was wrong.

Chapter 10

Adrian

I got back home that night feeling happier than I had in a long time. I felt like a shadow had come over my life since my mother's passing, a shadow that had drawn me back to Cañon City, but with Zoe's return to my life, that shadow was finally passing. I thought about that for a long time when I got back to Cañon Lodge. The house was quiet and still but enormous and empty too.

"You idiot," I muttered to myself as I stepped through the front door. "Why didn't you bring her home with you?" I didn't want Zoe to think I was shy and had certainly done enough to prove how physically attracted to her I was in the past. Happily, I thought back to only a few days ago when I had laid her out on the bed, quivering from the satisfaction I'd given her.

I poured a drink in my living room and relaxed by the fireplace before looking over my work for the week. I sipped my glass of scotch and relaxed, staring into the fire when an excellent thought danced right out of its flames and into my mind.

I knew that Zoe had an upcoming annual vacation—the

hospital was making her take it, as usual. Zoe never took her holiday properly, not wanting to leave any of her patients behind.

I could take her away. A proper vacation—the kind of thing Zoe would never normally afford or want for herself. It was the perfect idea. Happily, I pulled up my laptop from where it was on the coffee table. She'd told me when she was going to take her leave. I sent in my notice to HR, requesting the weekend that coincided with when she would be off.

Once that was done, I started looking for the place I wanted. I thought hard about what Zoe might like, a trip that would be really special for her and make her feel just the way I wanted her to feel—special.

I sat back once I'd booked the trip, watching the shadows playing around the stone wall of the living room. I watched them flicker and leap towards the window.

The window, where someone in black was standing.

I leaped to my feet, dropping my glass on the chair. "Hey!" I shouted. "Who's that!"

The figure turned and ran.

I sprinted up the corridor towards the front hall, where moonlight bathed the floors in gray, silvery tones. Fumbling with the door latch, I heard footsteps outside. Then the sound of a car door slamming and the motor starting.

I threw open the door, where I could already see a dark hatchback accelerating beyond the fence. Whoever the thief was, they'd hopped the nine-foot-tall stone wall that encircled the house and were almost at the main road down the hill and into Cañon. I ran down the driveway, over the smooth paving, and into the gravel, where my footsteps crunched as the car sped away. I was at the gate by the time the car finally vanished from sight, but even with my vision at 20/20, I couldn't see the car's license plate.

I stood there as I heard the engine firing in the distance. Whoever it was, they'd gotten away. I made a note of the car, a dark hatchback. I was going to have to tell the police.

What would I tell them?

That someone was trying to break into my house?

Who would be trying to rob me? I had a full security system in place; only someone highly skilled would have been able to find their way around it. No, whomever this person was, they were snooping around. They were spying, not stealing, from me. What surprised me most was that they hadn't triggered the alarm when they crossed the fence.

I went back inside and down the empty, echoing hallway. I could hear only my footsteps. But this time, I turned off to the left and descended into the basement. Behind the grey, concrete walls and a thick, heavy metal door was my security system. I checked the keypad on my way in and punched the code. It hadn't been unlocked. But when I got into the room and looked up at the banks of televisions, my heart skipped a beat.

The cameras were off, the screens dark or shaded in the fuzzy monochrome of static. I strode over to the computer and logged into the system. I opened the interface, and three words typed themselves onto the dark screen.

SYSTEM OFFLINE

>REBOOT?...

I typed the affirmative command into the keyboard, and the cameras turned back on. They weren't damaged, and the system was compromised. So how had the cameras managed to be turned off? There was no evidence on my camera feed that the car—or the person I'd seen outside the window—had ever been there. Someone had managed to disable the cameras.

I ran a routine scan on the system, checking for viruses or malware. It couldn't find anything. However the would-be intruder had hacked into my security system, they'd done it in such a way as to remain untraceable.

It was more than a little concerning. Normally these kinds of hacks were the work of serious criminals or rogue governments. But still, even if the cameras were offline, the motion sensors and laser detection system on the grounds should have activated the minute the thief jumped the fence.

A quick glance at the security system on my computer confirmed my suspicion. The system had been triggered to go offline between 10 and 11 pm. The cameras, on a closed-circuit loop, had been shut off. But whoever had broken the system had planned ahead. If I hadn't caught the thief, I might not have known about this until morning, when I left the house.

And in that time, anything could have happened.

I immediately sent an email to my security company to audit the system again and left a reminder for myself to call that damned detective, Vance, and let him know what had happened.

I thought about the car, the smashed window, keyed bonnet, and the graffiti.

I thought about what Charlie had told me, the complaints to FINRA and the SEC.

I stood there in the dark, hearing my heart pounding in the quiet of the night.

There was no doubt about it now.

Someone, somewhere, was trying to hurt me.

Chapter 11

Zoe

"Zoe?" called Clarissa from down the corridor.

"Just a sec," I called back. "I'll be back in a minute, Ellie."

"That's fine, dear." Eleanor May was sad I was going away for a few days. The damn hospital was making me take my vacation!

I walked down the corridor to the front desk of the cardiology department. Clarissa was on the phone. "I...I got you. She's right here. I'm sending her down, okay?"

Clarissa put the phone down. "Zoe, someone's here who says they're family."

"Who?" I replied. "Mom?"

"No, I saw Megan earlier," said Dr. Frisk from the other side of the desk, where he was filling in his logbook. "She's up in her office."

"No, it's a guy. I don't know. Says it's urgent. Wants to see you right away."

Weird. If it was my dad, why hadn't he called my mom? He

had my cell number, anyway. There'd be no need to show up at work. And if it was one of my aunts or uncles up in Denver, why hadn't they let me know they were coming down?

I rode the elevator down to the ground floor and turned left. I passed A&E and winced a little when I saw a kid with a broken foot. He was being lifted onto a stretcher. It looked pretty bad. I reminded myself to be grateful nothing like that had ever happened to me or my parents. Janice, a nurse from the oncology department, came past me. She'd probably been doing an MRI down in the basement.

"Zoe?" she said. "You okay?"

"I'm fine!" I said. "Someone's here to see me."

"Oh, okay!" she said. *Let's get coffee*, she mouthed, and I nodded and waved to her.

I went out the back to the employee parking lot. It was a warm day, and the sun was really beating down. We'd recently had the place tarmacked, and it was the fresh, sticky kind of black tarmac that gets hot in the sun.

"Hello!?" I called, a little nervous. No one answered. I looked around.

"Is someone here?" I said.

God, this is so weird, I thought to myself.

"Zoe!" said a familiar, reedy voice behind me.

I turned around to see Wesley.

He was dressed in black, still, but this time he'd at least put on shorts and a T-shirt. His wire-framed glasses were balanced a little askance on his nose like he'd been running to get here. In his right hand was his mobile phone. In his left, a bunch of yellow flowers. Wes had shown up to work to see me...with gas station daises?

"Wes?" I said, already uncomfortable. This was the last person I wanted to see at work. "What are you doing here?"

"I brought these!" said Wesley. "For you."

He held out the flowers to me.

"Oh," I said. "Well, thanks, I guess."

I didn't want to take the flowers, but he was holding them out insistently. Eventually, I took them, if only so I could hold them by my side.

"Wesley," I said.

"Yeah?" he replied. There was something eager and puppyish in his face, but he seemed kind of manic and overexcited to be here. "I wanted you to come down..." he said, "...so we could talk."

"What is it, Wesley?" I said, a growing feeling of dread in my stomach. *Was he about to ask me out again?* "What do you want?"

"So, is this where you work?"

This was the most surreal conversation I'd ever had. I was standing in the middle of a boiling parking lot, where my neighbor had lured me on the pretense of being a family member. And he was trying to make small talk.

"Wesley," I said. "Thank you for...for coming to see me, I guess. But Wes, I'm at work right now. Do you understand?"

He nodded but was still grinning like an idiot. I didn't think Wesley *did* understand.

"See, I can't really talk right now. I've got patients waiting for me. Do you understand?"

Wes looked disappointed, like I'd just rebuffed him. I could see his shoulders sink.

"Wesley," I said. "Why did you say you were a family member? That wasn't true."

"I just thought you'd come out to see me," he replied sulkily.

"If you lied?" I was angry, but I tried to be patient. Maybe he was just one of those people who needed life to be pointed out to them. "Wesley, you said it was an emergency. That wasn't very nice."

"So, does Adrian work here too?" said Wes. "Perhaps you could show me his office."

"No, Wes," I said, my temper rising. I had never lost my temper in my life, but this was exasperating. Wesley had come here on false pretenses, gotten me worried, and made me leave the ward while I was on shift, all to give me flowers and ask about Adrian. "That wouldn't be appropriate. It's inappropriate that you came here. Do you get that? Or..." I stopped myself from saying anything rude and backed away. "This isn't fair," I said. "Don't come here again. Do you understand?"

Wesley didn't say anything. I dropped the flowers on the ground and went back inside.

My nerves were shot. Something wasn't right with Wes. In the few months I'd gotten to know him since he moved in, I'd never felt this way about him. Sure, he was a little odd, and his personality and behavior would shift drastically sometimes, but not this. Never this. It felt almost...stalkerish. I needed to speak to someone. There was only one person that came to mind.

When I busted through the door of Adrian's office, he jumped up, startled. It was strange to see him rattled like that.

"You know Wesley? My neighbor?" I said without greeting.

"Oh, yeah," replied Adrian, forehead immediately tightening. "You talked to him today?"

"He came here," I said. "To see me."

Adrian looked suspicious, angry, even. Since I'd caught him spying on Wes when he asked me out at Adrian's house party, I knew he'd been jealous of Wes. But I was starting to think there was something else going on.

"What did he say?" said Adrian. I saw his jaw twitch. He was tense, angry, and protective, and it was more than a little attractive.

"He just started asking about the hospital. And you. He asked me to show you his office."

"That's really weird, Zoe," Adrian said. "You think he's okay? Seems crazy."

He paused while he waited for my answer, but as I was about to speak, Adrian looked up and interrupted me. "Does Wes have a dark hatchback?"

"Not a hatchback, no," I said, curious why he'd asked me that. "He's got a Hyundai. Why?"

Adrian looked thoughtful for a minute. "No reason," he said. "I just thought I might have seen his car around."

I knew he was keeping something from me, but I didn't push for the real reason behind his question. "Anyway, it was strange, creepy, and weird," I said.

"You're okay, Zoe," said Adrian as he stepped out from behind his desk. We were conscious that someone might knock on the door at any point, but I still wanted him to be near me, and I stepped closer, wanting the comfort of his touch, his kiss. "Look, there are always two nurses and a doctor on this floor, even at night. Everyone has to pass three checkpoints to get to the cardiology unit, and we have a full-time security team. You're safe at work, whatever this guy might want. Your place, however..."

"I don't think he'll do anything drastic. Maybe I'm just being overly cautious. He seems harmless enough," I said, stretching my hands around Adrian's broad shoulders. I rested my head on his chest, and we stood like that for a minute. "I just hope it's not my fault."

"It doesn't sound like it," said Adrian. "Look, there's something I want to discuss with you."

"What is it?" I asked.

"Tomorrow, you're on leave for a few days. Well, on the weekend, so am I."

I looked up at him. "Is that right?" A smile began to play on my lips. "You sly bastard!" I said. "You arranged it so we'd be on vacation together!"

Adrian laughed. It was so good to see him laugh. Most of the time, he was such a sourpuss, but when Adrian laughed, his voice was deep, and he opened his mouth, and the sight of it moved me in ways I could hardly explain.

"You got me," he said. "I've been thinking about us taking it slow."

"Oh?" I said innocently.

"Yeah. I've been thinking that maybe we shouldn't take it slow. Maybe we should go away together for a few days."

"Oh, Adrian!" I hadn't been on a proper vacation for well over a year. "Where are you taking me?"

"Well, that, of course, is a surprise. I thought you'd probably want to see your parents, maybe hang out with Giulia tomorrow." I stamped my foot and petulantly stuck my tongue out.

"No fair!"

Adrian grinned. "But on Friday, I thought maybe you'd like to come away with me for a day. Call it a weekend break."

"That's so sweet of you. I can't believe you'd do that for me."

Adrian shrugged. "No more than you deserve, sweetheart. Anyway, I'm not telling you where I'm going..." I folded my arms when I heard this, but he laughed again and uncrossed them. "But you should bring swimwear. All of it."

This was the most exciting news ever. A trip away with Adrian Lawson...my heart was already racing so that it hardly seemed anything but natural when he tipped my head towards him and kissed me right there in his office.

His kiss knocked me off balance. I thought I was going to fall, but Adrian's arms enclosed around me, and he pulled me towards him. I kissed back, throwing my hands around his neck into the soft, thick waves of his hair. I felt him growl a little as his mouth explored mine, happy with his prize.

Eventually, we broke off, and I stood there, palms pressed to his chest, feeling the well-defined pecs of my hot, billionaire doctor...what? Boyfriend? Even though we hadn't made it official, it felt right to think of him as my boyfriend.

"I'll see you at the airport on Friday afternoon, okay?" he said.

"You're the best," I said, sighing happily. My fears had been forgotten.

Chapter 12

Adrian

I wanted to take Zoe to New Mexico. Even in my Chevy, driving there would have been a little long, so I arranged a private flight for us.

Zoe was amazed when the plane taxied out onto the runway, ready to reach us. Contrary to what most people thought, I didn't actually own a private jet. I thought it would be a waste of money when I hardly ever traveled outside the United States anyway. I was so busy working in medicine that I hardly ever took vacations, so I was looking forward to getting away with Zoe myself.

However, while I didn't own a plane, I knew plenty of people who did. My friend Steve, the CEO of a large pharmaceutical company I invested several million dollars in, kindly allowed me to borrow his HondaJet for the weekend. It was a sleek, modern aircraft with angular wingtips and engines mounted over, rather than under, its wings. It allowed for a smoother ride, and once we'd taken off, to Zoe's delight, I held her hand for a little while before opening a bottle of champagne.

"To a lovely weekend," I ventured. She chinked her glass gently against mine and took a sip.

About an hour later, we were touching down in the desert in the middle of New Mexico. I had a car there waiting to meet us for the twenty minutes or so it would take us to drive up into the mountains. Eventually, after we drifted through vistas so beautiful they took my breath away, we arrived at *El Asiento del Alma.*

El Asiento del Alma, or 'The Seat of the Soul,' was an enormous hotel and spa retreat. Built in the mission style, it sat about halfway between White Sands and El Paso, isolated and inaccessible to all but the most exclusive clients. It was expensive to book, and I'd had to grease the wheels of commerce to get us there at short notice, but I was confident that once we were secluded from everything, it would be worth it. And Zoe was going to have the time of her life—I wanted to make sure of that.

We were dropped off at the resort amidst a garden full of colonial pavers and exquisite fountains. In the center of the elegantly sculpted, geometrically pleasing garden was a stone sculpture of Cupid and Venus. A stunning display of water jets came from the goddess of love's outstretched palm and the cherub's feet. Ahead of us, across an expansive plaza and up a set of stone steps, was the hotel lobby.

As we crossed the plaza, a pair of hotel attendants dressed in white shirts and dark waistcoats came out to meet us. Alyssia, one of the hotel's hosts and our guide for the weekend, approached. She was dressed like a supervillain, wearing a dark linen jacket with a nehru collar, shirt, and jeans.

"Adrian!" she screeched. "Welcome back!"

"Hi, Alyssia," I said. "Zoe, this is Alyssia Brugel. She was top of my class at Johns Hopkins two years ago. I'm pleased to say she's the hotel's head physician."

"It's nice to meet you," Zoe said, stretching out her arms. Alyssia reached out and shook her hand in one firm motion.

"Dr. Lawson is our ideal client," she explained in her clipped, Swiss accent to Zoe as we entered. "He's one of the few clients whose medical knowledge allows him to appreciate what we're doing here..."

"And afford it, too," I smirked. Alyssia flashed her eyes at me and then turned as we entered the lobby.

It was pretty fabulous. The lobby was decorated in black marble, with more rushing fountains behind the check-in desk. Beyond that, a perfectly polished glass wall ran in a square around the hotel's courtyard, where couples wandered dreamily. The cult-like atmosphere of the resort was initially a little intimidating. The reason I'd wanted to bring Zoe here, however, was because *El Asiento* offered the best spa treatment in the world.

"This is amazing," said Zoe. "How long's it been here?"

"The building we're in has been standing here for almost two hundred years," explained Alyssia. "It was one of the first Catholic monasteries to be built on this land. The parent company of the spa acquired the land seven years ago. Since then, it's been a private resort for only the most exclusive clientele."

Zoe was wide-eyed as a little kid who had been taken to Disneyland, and I loved it. I squeezed her hand, and she looked at me, kissing me on the cheek. "You're really something," she said.

"Your bags are already in your room, which is on the second floor," explained Alyssia. "I've booked you in for dinner at 7 pm. There are a lot of treatments scheduled for tomorrow—you guys are having the works. Balneotherapy, including mud bath or *heubad*, your choice..."

"Hay," I explained to Zoe. "That's getting bathed in hay."

"As in, like..." Zoe said slowly, "...what farm animals eat?"

I nodded, and we both tried not to giggle.

"...Massage, tai chi, energy meditation—not a practice I am fond of, mind you, if you ask me, it's purely pseudoscientific...."

The list of treatments went on until, eventually, Alyssia Brugel vanished around the corner, lost in monologue.

"Do they have a pool?" said Zoe.

I laughed, and she laughed too—after she punched me in the arm!

*

Dinner was incredible. Zoe and I could hardly pronounce any items on the menu, but the restaurant itself was an amazing cross between an ultra-healthy spa café and a Michelin-starred restaurant. I had mackerel, with an elegant salad of confit tomatoes and a smooth sauce laced with delicious caviar. Zoe had a keto salad with walnuts, gorgonzola, and silky, dressed green leaves, sprinkled with flowers.

Our room, too, was amazing. It was more of an apartment, really, with a lounge, main bedroom, and enormous wetroom together. It opened onto an expansive open balcony. Zoe was confused about a small door next to the main bedroom.

"Is that a closet?" she asked. "Where does it go?"

"Oh, it goes to a personal attendant's quarters."

"Personal attendant? You mean like a servant, right?"

I had to admit, it was ridiculous.

After dinner, we took a walk around the hotel gardens. "I'm

amazed," said Zoe. "It's like there's a whole secret world out there, as long as you can afford it."

"I had to go through that when I made my money," I replied. "You start wondering what you can actually do with your resources. Turns out there's a whole world of things to do—if you know where to look."

"I don't think I could ever get used to your lifestyle," said Zoe. "The fast cars, the hotels, the vacations."

"I've been lucky," I admitted. "If I were just a normal cardiologist, I wouldn't be able to have half as much of this."

"And yet..." said Zoe, "...you dedicate your time to saving lives and treating people when you don't have to work at all. That's pretty special, Adrian. You have to admit that."

When most people complimented me, I tended to shrug them off. It was different when Zoe complimented me. I felt almost bashful. I didn't know what to say when she confessed to admiring me. It was amazing how we'd gone from being enemies to this so quickly.

"Come on," I said. "It's late."

*

The *banya* was an old Russian kind of spa treatment. Initially, Zoe thought it sounded pretty fun. "Go and sit in a steam room before breakfast?" she said the next morning after we arrived. "That sounds pretty good."

But when we got there, and the attendant explained what would happen next, her eyes widened.

"They *whip* you?" she said. "What is this, some kind of kinky sex club?"

"No, no," I explained, but I was almost overcome with giggles. "They lightly whack you with branches. Then, you take a dip in the ice bath."

"Branches? *ICE BATH?*" Zoe looked like she was about to bolt. "I think I just want my breakfast, thank you."

"Trust me," I said. "You won't regret it."

The atmosphere in the sauna grew pretty tense, but we had no idea what they had in store for us. Eventually, our names were called.

"Oh Lord," said Zoe. "Maybe I should have got some fetish gear before I went to the crazy billionaire resort hotel."

The 'whipping' was pretty luxurious. We both stretched out on a pair of soft massage benches, where a pair of attendants arrived to give us a quick rub down. Then, the branches came out. Zoe initially squealed, but after a while, the beating started to become pleasant, even ticklish.

"Damn," she said. "I could get used to this."

"Okay," said one of the masseuses. "Which of you is going in first?"

"Oh hell," said Zoe. "Not me."

"I guess it's my turn!" I said.

The ice bath was out of the door and to the left. In modern indoor *banyas*, it was usually just a pool of cold-ish water. Here, though, at *El Asiento*, they used crushed ice. "Take a deep breath, and jump when you're ready," said the attendant.

The pool wasn't enormous—maybe ten feet by twelve—but it was deep. Seriously deep. The idea was to totally submerge yourself. "I guess this will be an interesting medical experiment,"

I said and dived in.

GOD DAMN!

The water was cold. Colder than cold. I felt like my entire body was on fire with the icy craziness of the pool. As I fell under the surface, I felt a rushing intake of breath involuntarily sucked water into my mouth, and I could already feel myself shuddering and shivering as I broke the surface of the water. I gasped and let out a resounding cry as I reached for air. It must have sounded like I'd been taken into a torture chamber to Zoe, who was still sitting in the warmth of the steam rooms at the back. Slowly, I climbed out of the pool, and two of the attendants arrived and toweled me down before I caught hypothermia.

"The things I do for my health," I said, panting.

Unbelievably, though, it worked. It *more* than worked. I felt *great*. The extremes of heat and temperature were amazingly good for my circulation. After I'd calmed down, my heart rate slowed, and I felt euphoric and relaxed. The effect was temporary, but I was amazed at how pleasurable the sensations of the *banya* were.

"That was really something," said Zoe as we sat on the terrace of the resort restaurant an hour later for breakfast. I was having oatmeal with flax seeds, granola, fresh fruit, and cream. Zoe had insisted on steak and eggs. "I've been boiled, scoured, whipped, and frozen in ice water. I'm healthy enough," she had told the waiter, who smiled and ran inside to ask the chef what could be done about it.

"It's incredible that you did it," I said. "I thought you were going to run out of the room screaming when they told you about the ice bath."

"Are you kidding? I love trying new things!" said Zoe, finishing her breakfast and pushing the plate away. "Admittedly, the new things are usually, like, a different way of doing my hair or finding a book I haven't read before for Mr. McCabe. But Russian spa treatments will do!"

"Are you ready to get bathed in hay, then?" I said, leaning across the table and looking deep into her blue eyes. Zoe was beautiful. There was no doubt about it. And the healthy glow the *banya* had given her skin made me ravenous for her. I longed to touch her skin and kiss her again, and after our first, chaste night in the hotel, Zoe seemed to want me just the same.

"Tell you what," she said in a low, husky voice that meant trouble. "How about we go back to the room first?"

Chapter 13

Zoe

As soon as we got back to the room, I knew I'd never be able to keep my hands off him. In the beautiful morning light that streamed through our window, I slowly unbuttoned Adrian's shirt and removed it, my eyes drawn to his soft, olive-bronzed skin. I'd always loved that faintly exotic look of his, and now, in this beautiful paradise he'd brought me to, his body was here for me to enjoy.

I kissed his collarbone and his chest, hearing his soft sighs as my mouth moved gently downwards. I bent low and kissed his well-defined and sharp abs before dropping to my knees.

"Doctor," I whispered. "You seem a little stressed at the moment. I can feel your heart pounding, and you seem to have shortness of breath. Perhaps I can help relax you?"

Adrian shivered, and a chuckle escaped his lips as I unzipped his pants and let them fall, along with his underwear, to his ankles. I greedily eyed his erect, throbbing cock and let my hands run down from his pecs all the way to his dick. I gently put my hands around the shaft and slowly began to stroke, working it, feeling it swell to its full, intimidatingly large size in my hands. Adrian moaned gently, and I felt his legs tense.

"Well, that's not good," I replied. "You're just getting more excited. I might have to use my mouth..."

"You just might," he gasped in reply, one of his hands beginning gently to weave its way through my hair. I loved the feeling of his hands on me, passionate, controlling, desperate. It was like I'd finally found an outlet for all that rudeness and anger. *Possess me, Adrian, control me*, I thought to myself. *Let it all out.*

I couldn't stop myself any longer, and slowly, tenderly, I kissed his cock, letting it slide past my lips until I had him in my mouth. I looked up at him with my best big, blue doe eyes, and he looked back approvingly, smiling. I began first to lick, then to suck, trying to take as much of him in as possible.

"Zoe," he whispered, and hearing my name only made me feel more delighted, more special. I continued to dutifully suck Adrian's dick, enjoying the occasional spasms of pleasure coursing through his body that I felt with delight through my hands and mouth.

"Slow down, princess," he said, and I did so, stopping to look up at him.

"Something wrong?" I said, wiping my mouth daintily.

"Yeah," he said. "I'm not inside of you."

Adrian bent down and pulled me to my feet, and I giggled as he wrestled with me, jealously, possessively. Within no time at all, he'd pushed me onto the enormous, king-sized bed of the hotel room and was busy pulling off my clothes at an alarming rate. Once he'd stripped me bare, Adrian cupped my breast with his hand while the other held my face and kissed me deeply. I could feel his cock had grown even more now, that it was as hard as I'd ever made it, and he was about to put it inside me. At the thought, spontaneously, I felt a flood of desire course through me, opening me to him. But first, he just teased me with the tip.

"Come on," I said. "I want it. I do."

"Yeah?" he growled in that deep voice. God, his voice had always been deep for his age. Even back when he was a teenager, just a word from him had rumbled through me.

"You gonna give it to me, or what?" I said. When I dated guys, I never had the confidence to talk like this. I'd never felt so passionate about someone that I could ask for what I wanted. I didn't know what I was going to do if I couldn't have Adrian right here, right now.

So when he gave himself to me, it felt like heaven.

Finally, he thrust into me, and I gasped, tensing a little at the sheer size of him. But gradually, gently, he worked his way inside until he was thrusting into me with all the enthusiasm I expected of my gorgeous Italian stallion!

I tightened my legs around his waist and purred, moaning with every deep, slow thrust he made, his dick sending shockwaves of pleasure through my legs, up around my waist, and my spine. His strength held me in place, and I surrendered to it happily as he made his way into me with greater and greater force until I felt him touching a part of me I'd never known before.

By angling himself upwards, Adrian stimulated me in just the right place, and I practically wailed with the sheer ecstasy of it. I'd never been with a man so big he could satisfy me like that, and it shocked me, sending me off balance. "Don't stop," I heard myself say, "don't stop," before, finally, I felt him withdraw.

"No...no," I moaned pathetically, robbed of the orgasm I'd felt rushing to completion. But Adrian had other ideas.

"Sit up. Turn around," he said. I blushed at the strength he commanded me with but obeyed his will, turning myself around on my hands and knees while he entered me from behind.

If I thought he'd been fucking me hard before, I wasn't even remotely prepared for what Adrian had to show me next. He fucked me quickly, without mercy, as I smiled and bent over, letting my head rest on the pillow and my hand finding its way instinctively between my legs. "Good girl," he whispered as I began to stimulate my clit, touching myself while he fucked me harder, faster than I knew he could.

Within no time at all, I was coming for him, yelping as my knees buckled with the sheer intensity of it before Adrian came too, flooding me with pleasure. He withdrew himself from my trembling hips and flopped down on the bed next to me, where we lay for a while, panting and gasping with astonishment.

"How are you enjoying your vacation?" he said, lazily stroking my hair as I rested my head on his chest.

"Just fine." I smiled dizzily as my heart rate began to return to normal.

"Mhh..." He snuggled into my neck. "I aim to please. And I'm not done yet."

Oh...

*

Sunday was bittersweet.

I let Adrian take me for a walk around the gardens, but the truth was I'd have let him ravish me again if my body could have taken it. The sun began to shine brighter there in the mountains, and as the temperature grew, I found myself flushing spontaneously as a host of happy hormones started to drive me crazy. I felt so safe and secure in Adrian's presence, and he'd done such a nice thing by bringing me out here to a place I'd never normally have had the chance to go. So by the time we had to leave and get our flight back to Cañon City, I felt a little melancholy.

We drove back down to the airstrip, where the plane was waiting for us. As we climbed onboard, Adrian sighed. "I've got so much work to do…" he said, "…but I'd rather just stay here and hold your hand." I grinned and rested my head on his shoulder as we took off. I took a nap on the plane—who wouldn't, after what he'd done to me in that hotel room all of yesterday and twice this morning—but I woke up as we were coming down into Colorado airspace.

"You know," I said, "Giulia's probably wondering where we've both gone off to."

"I was thinking about that."

"She's probably wondering if we're with each other."

"I know."

"Which is going to be confusing because she thinks we don't get on that well."

"I don't know about that."

"Adrian!" I said. He was teasing me with short, ambivalent answers. "Come on. What are we gonna tell her?"

Adrian growled. "I'll tell her I was out of town taking care of my investments. Hell, I should be…" he muttered, his expression darkening a little. What did he mean by that?

"And what will I say?" I responded.

"You're not exactly the best liar. Maybe you'll just have to tell her the truth."

"The truth?" I balked. "But, I can't..."

"Not the whole truth." Adrian winked at me, lightness and humor returning to his features. "Tell her you were with a guy."

"Oh yeah?" I said. "And what will I say about this mystery guy? She's gonna be all over me with questions."

"Not sure. But you can do it. I trust you."

I have to admit, his answers disappointed me a little. I was hoping Adrian would say that we'd need to tell Giulia. Now that he'd taken me away for a weekend, I thought maybe we'd acknowledge how serious things were. I mean, it wasn't like a casual thing...was it? I wasn't really sure anymore. Taking me for dinner—even a romantic, lamplit dinner in the desert—was pretty different from a weekend away at an exclusive spa resort. It was like we were a couple now. Not telling Giulia seemed like a bad idea. But I didn't say anything because I didn't want to push him.

We touched down outside of Cañon City at 5 pm. The shadows were growing longer, and as I stepped out, I felt the warm air from the plane replaced by a slight, almost imperceptible chill.

"You know," I said as we walked to the car on the airstrip. "We still have tomorrow off from work, even if you have stuff to do. We can do something."

"How about you spend the night at mine?" said Adrian. "I have a bigger TV. And there's a swimming pool. Though it isn't ice-cold like the *banya* one, I'm afraid."

"No problem!" I said, and we laughed as Adrian opened the door for me and held it.

I was excited at all the things we'd be able to do that evening. Adrian had introduced me to the pleasures of luxury resort spas, but I was interested in seeing what he did when he was alone at home. *He probably reads long books about medicine and fintech*, I thought, watching his stern, handsome profile in the setting sun as we both sat in the backseat of the car.

As we climbed the hill that led up to Adrian's mansion, though, I heard him hold his breath and saw his posture stiffen.

"What's wrong?" I asked as we rounded the final corner of the driveway.

"Stop," Adrian said. "Stop the car. Now."

Chris, the driver, pulled to a halt, and Adrian stepped out. I leaned out to see what he was looking at, but he slammed the car door, and I jumped. I undid my seatbelt and got out of my own side.

Over the roof of the car, I saw Adrian standing in the driveway. He was looking up at the gate of the mansion.

Or, where the gate should have been.

A torn, twisted hunk of metal was lying in the driveway where the gate should have been. It had been rammed and fallen off its hinges, where it lay on the ground.

Beyond the dark, handsome man who stood before me, I could see all the way up to the house, up the steps to its porch and the enormous, wooden doors.

They were left open.

While we were away, Adrian's house had been robbed.

Chapter 14

Adrian

"I know what you're saying, Dr. Lawson," drawled Vance as he chewed a stick of gum. The detective was holding his hat in one hand while the other scratched his head. "But I just can't see how this can be anything other than a simple burglary."

I suppressed a sigh of exasperation as we stood in the driveway. "That gate..." I said, "...was locked magnetically. Whoever rammed the driveway did it with an enormous truck. They were trying to damage the property, not steal anything."

Vance looked at me with his beady eyes and carried on chewing his gum. I was well aware of what his slow, confident, unassuming stare meant. The guy was trying to psych me out and intimidate me. I wasn't buying it for a second.

"There you go again," muttered Vance, "playing criminologist with me."

"I'm not playing," I said.

"Well, Dr. Lawson," interrupted Vance, "it would be pretty useful if you could provide me with your security camera footage.

Or any of the information from the sensors you claim to have on the property. I'd imagine Officer Clark already asked you for that. I'm confused as to why you're not handing it over."

"I'm not handing it over," I said, almost gritting my teeth, "because it isn't there. That's what I'm telling you. Someone's disabled the system." Even after the security company had tightened the loopholes in my system after the intruder with the hatchback, somehow, my system had been compromised *again*.

"Really," said Vance, without curiosity. "Someone here had the know-how to disable your high-tech fancy-pants security system? All just to ram down your gate and destroy your front door?"

I shook my head. "Not just that. They've found my safe. Someone did try to rob me. But they weren't interested in taking computers or TVs. They were interested in something else. Something they thought I kept in that safe."

"And what do you keep in that safe?" said Vance disinterestedly.

"It's *private*," I said. The truth was, I didn't keep much of anything in there. I kept some mementos and things of my mother's in there and a hard drive of my personal data from the past ten years or so of investing. But I didn't see why someone would try and steal that when most of the valuable information was stored on my portfolio manager, Charlie's, server. It would have been easier to try and hack that than to break into the house. Less chance of getting caught, too.

"Look, I don't keep much of anything in there," I tried to explain.

"I understand," Vance said slightly. "A wealthy, important man like you has plenty of secrets to protect."

"*No*," I said, beginning to lose my temper. "I don't. I'm a legitimate businessman with no record of trouble with the law or unscrupulous dealings."

"Right," said Vance. "Dr. Lawson, may I ask you something?"

"Sure," I said.

"Has your financial operation, the stocks in New York, I mean, received any complaints recently?"

I wanted to groan internally.

"How do you know about that?" I said.

Vance smiled again, a humorless smile. "It's my job to know about people's business, *Adriano*. If I may call you by your first name. It's my job to know what's going on. Whether, for example, someone's been accused of committing serious financial crimes."

"Those allegations are false and have been submitted to slander me," I said desperately. "And that's completely beside the point. Someone has attacked my house and disabled the security system in order to do so. I want you to find them."

Vance looked at the ground and shook his head. "I'll do my best to investigate this incident, *Adriano*," he said. I didn't like the way he said my name with the vaguest sneer. "But I want you to consider the possibility that you forgot to turn on the system before you left the house to...go to where exactly?"

"A spa weekend," I said.

"Was that with...Miss Hollis, here?" said Vance. His eyes drifted over to where Zoe was sitting fifty yards away on the steps as a crowd of police officers walked in and out of the house.

I looked at him. If I told Vance, then someone knew our secret, and there was no way we'd be able to hide it from Giulia—or Zoe's mom—for very long. My reputation would be at risk. On the other hand, if I lied, it would make me look even more guilty to Vance.

"I don't know what I've done to offend you, detective," I said slowly. "I just want you to know that I'm seriously considering filing a complaint to the city council about your personal treatment of me." *Now you've done it.* My mother had always told me off for my temper. *Fuoco,* she called me when I got angry. *Fire.* I saw why now because Vance seemed to relax.

He didn't tense or stiffen up like I'd imagined. And then my heart sank as I realized that he'd wanted me to lose my temper and say something like that.

"Dr. Lawson," Vance continued, returning his notebook to his pocket and putting away his pen, "whatever would you have to complain about?"

"Firstly, my car. Someone broke into my house and vandalized it. Now my house has been broken into, and the state-of-the-art security system has been disabled. You can't 'forget to turn it on,'" I said, gesturing at the house to make my point. "It's always on. I can view the cameras myself. I'll bet you they were turned off an hour before—"

I froze. *Just like the night I'd seen the man at my window.*

Vance looked at me. He wasn't smiling anymore. In fact, he looked bored. And there was something sinister about his boredom, as though he'd known the conversation was coming to this point and had been waiting for me to catch up.

"Mr. Lawson, I need to go now before I waste any more of my time. All I'll say is this..." he said, as he turned his back on me, "...I can only help people who help themselves. And you are not helping yourself right now."

He strode away. "Wrap it up soon, guys," he called to the officers.

By the time the sun had finally set, the police had left, and I was alone on the steps of my house, in front of the shattered door next to Zoe.

*

"I just have one question." Zoe was looking at me as we sat in the living room.

"Yeah?" I looked up from the glass of scotch I'd poured myself, and my eyes stared into the hearth. I hadn't bothered to light the fire, so we were talking by the light of the heavy reading lamp.

"Why didn't you call the cops when you saw that guy through the window?"

I shifted uncomfortably in my chair. "I don't know," I said. "I guess, I just..."

I looked into all the dark corners of the room, searching for a threat that wasn't there. Whoever my enemy was, they'd vanished into thin air like smoke.

"I guess I didn't call them for a couple of reasons," I said. "The first being that somehow I always expected this."

"What?" said Zoe. She was confused.

"I mean," I explained, "that my mother brought us to America when I was very young. Right after my father died. She never really told us about where we came from or my family. We were never meant to go back and find it out. I mean, we're Italian, for God's sake. What kind of woman doesn't rely on her family in her time of need?"

Zoe looked at me. "I don't know," she replied. "A woman on the run from something, maybe?"

That thought chilled me down to my bones. Zoe was right. Had whatever chased my mother out of Italy also returned to haunt me? The thought made me afraid for me, Giulia, and anyone else caught up in my life. Zoe included.

"I don't know what to think anymore." I pinched my eyes. "That guy Vance is a real jerk. Does your dad know him at all?"

Zoe shrugged her shoulders. "Sure, but not like as friends or anything. I guess he must make depositions in court now and then. Not that the crime rate's that high here. He only moved here a few months ago; I know that for certain."

I narrowed my eyes. "A few months ago? Like, when I was appointed director of cardiology at the hospital?"

Zoe sighed and rubbed her cheeks. "How should I know Adrian?"

"Maybe you could ask your mom when they had the board meeting to approve my appointment..."

"No," said Zoe. "I'm not doing that. She always makes me feel like I should be working harder than everyone else so everyone knows I didn't just get a job at Cañon Hospital because of her. It isn't fair already. Lord knows what she'll say if I ask her for information about the board of trustees."

"Come on, Zoe."

"I said no, Adrian. Look, can't we just have a nice end to the weekend? Don't spoil things by—"

"By what, Zoe?" I said. "My house is trashed. The door's broken in. What do you expect me to do?"

"I don't know! Just come here and..."

"No." My temper had gotten the better of me. I looked at the empty fireplace. *Fuoco.* Just like Mama said...

"Just go home, Zoe," I said. "It's not safe here. I'll call you a cab."

I stood up and marched out of the room. She didn't argue.

Chapter 15

Zoe

It was the first time Adrian had made me cry since he'd come back to Cañon City, and I promised myself it would be the last. How could I have been so stupid to pretend that I could trust him?

Ever since I'd first met him, I'd wanted to get to know him better, wanted to share more of the details of his life. But things constantly got in the way, whether it was other boys or his grumpy personality. And now something was happening that I didn't understand, something which was clearly causing him trouble...

And he had pushed me away so easily.

I went to bed that night in tears. Gone was the magic of the weekend, the amazing romantic energy that had existed between us at the resort. I felt like I'd been on an enormous high, and now I was finally coming down.

I woke up on Monday morning feeling a little tired after all the excitement from last night. I was worried about Adrian, and my first thought that morning was to text him before I'd gotten up or showered. I reached for my phone, wanting to send a message.

Then, I stopped myself.

I don't know why I didn't text him. I guess I felt it was his turn to apologize.

Instead, I got up and fixed myself some breakfast. I only had one day left before I was back on shift tomorrow at the hospital—a grueling series of days and nights. I decided to make the most of it. And I was wondering how when I heard someone ring the doorbell.

At first, I thought it must be Adrian. *He's come to apologize.* But I was hardly less pleased when I opened it and saw Giulia standing there, looking excited about something.

"Hi, bestie!" she said, then stepped through the doorway, grabbing me by the collar playfully.

"*What. Is. His. Name?*" she said and giggled.

I laughed nervously. *Of course, she'd guess I was with someone.* I'd predicted it on the plane ride home from the resort the previous day. But now, as I looked into Giulia's smiling face, an uncomfortable thought dawned on me. I wouldn't be able not to share my secrets with Giulia—she was my best friend. But I knew Adrian didn't want me to tell her what had happened. And how would I explain to her about the break-in?

If Giulia didn't already know that Adrian's house had been broken into, I knew she'd want to hear it as soon as possible. But if I told her, she'd know I'd been there last night. I was trapped. I hadn't thought about how deeply I'd gotten involved with Adrian. Neither had I considered that Giulia, as much as it pained me, was going to find out sooner or later.

"Oh...you know," I said, feigning a smile.

"Come on! I want details, sister! Tell me everything. What's his name? And did you guys go away somewhere or what? I've been ringing your doorbell since Friday night."

I laughed a little nervously, but it was hard to know what to say. "I'll tell you what I got up to this weekend," I said coyly, "after you tell me what we're doing today."

Giulia punched me gently on the arm—though gentle for Giulia was pretty hard. "No fair!" she said. "Still, maybe you'll open up when Wesley gets here."

Wesley? She'd invited him over?

"Oh, you did?" I hadn't mentioned Wes' weird appearance at work to Giulia or the super-confusing revelation he'd made to me at Adrian's housewarming. I guess Giulia thought we were still friendly neighbors. Besides, I didn't want to make Wes feel uncomfortable.

"Great," I said weakly. "What's the plan?"

"Well, I thought we'd take him to the museum first, you know. I bet Wes will love all that dinosaur stuff. And then we can go out for ice cream?"

"Sounds good," I said. If Giulia hadn't already invited Wes, I'd have asked her not to bring him. As much as I wanted to forgive him, I couldn't help but feel creeped out by his presence.

But through the screen door, I could already see him, a monochrome shadow pacing across my lawn in the bright sunlight.

*

We were sitting around my kitchen table, getting ready to go out, when Giulia excused herself to use the bathroom. I winced internally and waited until she'd left.

Alone in the room with Wes, I was nervous. I hadn't seen him since his strange, creepy appearance at the hospital last week. And if that wasn't enough to freak me out, I already knew that Wes liked me more than just as a friend. In the silence of the room, I could hear my kitchen clock ticking a little as beads of sweat began to gather on Wes' temple. He hadn't looked at me since Giulia left the room.

"You settling in fine?" I said, making small talk.

"Sure," Wes said, looking into his lap. "My yard's looking nice. And I've got plenty of furniture for the house now. And work's going pretty well."

"That sounds great," I said. Wes seemed totally relaxed, which was nice. And he was more relaxed than usual. Super-relaxed, actually.

"How are you?" Wes returned.

"Oh, me?" I didn't want to tell him too much, but it would have killed me not to be polite.

"Things going well with your guy-friend?"

I smiled and looked away. "That's kinda private, Wes," I said slowly, with a low voice. Inside I was practically screaming for him to shut up.

Why did Giulia have to say anything the minute he walked in?

"Sorry. I didn't mean any offense."

"No, I'm sorry, that was...that was rude, Wes. I apologize."

"Look, Zoe..." He sighed. "I get it. You aren't interested in me. It's fine. I'm over it. I just want us to move on and be friends."

I looked up at him. Wes seemed pretty serious. His posture was open, and he sat up straight, confidently, looking me in the eye.

"That's really nice of you, Wes. I want to be friends too. It's just...it's complicated, and I don't really want to talk about who I'm seeing...or, God forbid, introduce him to anyone just yet."

Wes nodded. "I understand. It can be difficult, you know. Especially if you guys aren't getting along."

I felt a slightly uneasy feeling in the pit of my stomach. "How do you know...I mean, what makes you say we're not getting along?"

"I know you and Adrian are together, Zoe. And I know you had a fight last night."

My eyes must have doubled in size at that point. I heard a tiny gasp escape my throat, and I stood up, wanting to leave the room. But as I did, Wes leaned over in one, sudden, smooth motion and wrapped his hand around my wrist. He looked up into my eyes.

"He's no good for you, Zoe."

Upstairs, I heard Giulia humming a tune. I looked into Wes' eyes. They seemed empty, like there was nothing in them.

"*Acqua in bocca,*" he said. "When she comes down."

What?

"What did you just say?"

"*Acqua in bocca.* It's an Italian expression. It means keep your mouth shut."

Silence and something akin to fear engulfed me. Wes' mouth was twisted into a sneer. But when Giulia entered, he let go of my wrist and was back to the Wes we knew.

It's all a façade.

"Ready to go?"

I backed away and left the room. "You guys go without me," I heard myself say through the shock permeating my whole system.

Chapter 16

Adrian

"You're an idiot," I said, looking at myself in the mirror.

I'd called Zoe five times that Monday, or tried to, but she hadn't picked up at any point. I was sitting at the desk in my office. It had cost twenty thousand dollars to get the door fixed at such short notice, and I was writing the check when the phone rang. I grabbed my phone, anxiously wanting to see Zoe's name appear on the screen. But it wasn't her. Of course. Why would she call me now, after how I'd treated her last night?

I pressed the button and put the phone to my ear. "Charlie," I said listlessly. It had been a sleepless night, and I was tired and in no mood to talk about it.

"Sorry for bothering you..." Charlie said, "...but I need you to review all this with me before tomorrow's meeting. Our partners are obviously concerned. The size and scale of these complaints, Adrian...If I didn't know better, I'd say someone was deliberately trying to cause us trouble."

"What if they are?" I said suddenly. There was a shocked silence at the end of the phone.

"You really think that someone might be targeting you personally?"

"I don't know what I think. Not right now. But I do know that I'm not going to stand by while they do this to me. Whoever they are."

"Adrian, I've been in this business for twenty years. I'm also one of the best at it. And I've worked with some impressive characters. Few of them were as rich as you, but almost all of them..." Charlie chuckled, "...were more crooked. Can I give you some advice? As a friend?"

"Sure," I said. "I'm willing to hear anything."

I could hear Charlie taking a deep breath on the other end of the line. "We need to assume, for now," said Charlie, "that whoever's lodged these complaints has a legitimate grievance."

"What?" I said, annoyed. "But they don't. Charlie, you look after the fund. You know as well as I do that there's no evidence at all."

"With every portfolio as large as yours," Charlie continued, "there are gaps I can't fill. Aspects of the fund I'm not as familiar with as others. Find me someone who can account for every cent you have invested in this thing, and I'll find you a liar. You're one of the more complicated private investors in the history of modern banking, Adrian. Believe me."

I sighed, frustrated. "So, what are you saying?" I said slowly. "That you think I've been cooking the books from a doctor's office while you sit there and play pawn to my Ponzi schemes?"

"No," said Charlie. "But, if there's anything you have to tell me...if there's anything anyone could pin on you, now's the time."

"There's nothing," I said firmly. "*Nothing*. Do you hear me?"

There was silence on the phone.

"For your sake," said Charlie, "I hope you're right. Because believe me, I've got the IRS coming in on Friday, and if I can't find something, I'm sure they will. I just..." he paused.

"Just what?" I huffed, impatient.

"I just hope that you know that if someone's doing this to you, they must really hate you, man. Do you know how serious the penalties are for falsely alleging financial conduct? Whoever launched these allegations is up to lose millions of dollars if we prove them wrong."

"Which we will," I said. "Charlie, listen. I'm sorry for getting angry. I had a break-in here last night."

"A break-in?" said Charlie.

"Nothing was taken, but they tried to crack my safe. They were after *something*, that's for sure."

Both Charlie and I knew that the complaints that had been filed against me through FINRA and the IRS couldn't possibly be unconnected with it. I hadn't wanted to tell him, but it seemed like the only way to gain his trust—to make him believe that I was being investigated for no good reason.

"I'm sorry. I had no idea."

"It's fine. Call me tomorrow and tell me how it goes. I trust you."

"I appreciate that. Good afternoon, Adrian."

I put the phone down on my desk and looked up into the mirror on the opposite wall. Someone was trying to make me lose my trust in others. I wouldn't let that happen.

*

I went into the hospital early the following day. I'd almost finished my admin for the day, which was good. I had a scheduled triple bypass at 2 pm, two consultations, a meeting with the board of directors, and the daily cycle of ward rounds to get through. My day was busy. I stayed at my desk most of the morning, planning my week and preparing for what lay ahead.

I was looking forward to seeing Zoe running around in the corridors of the cardiology department, helping patients, and talking to the staff.

But when I got there, I was surprised to see that Zoe's name wasn't on the rotation board anymore.

"Dr. Frisk?" I called him over.

"What can I do for you, Dr. Lawson?" he said. Frisk was giving me a funny look like something had gone wrong.

"I was just wondering where Nurse Hollis is this morning," I said, smiling. "Aren't we missing a dose of sunshine on this ward?"

Frisk frowned. "Zoe asked if she could swap shifts with Colleen last night so Colleen could go to her daughter's violin recital."

I nodded. "Sure thing, thanks."

Frisk nodded. He looked as if he was about to leave, then spoke, this time in a quieter voice, so none of the staff or patients around us could hear. "Hey, Adrian?"

"Yep?" I was confused. Normally Frisk was a cheerful, easygoing kind of fellow. But his mood was dark. Conspiratorial, even.

"I was wondering if I could speak to you in my office later. After I've done the rounds."

"Sure thing," I said. "Why don't I do them with you? Two heads are better than one, after all."

"Uh, no," said Frisk. "No, thank you. But I'll catch you later. You're in surgery at 2, right?"

"That's right," I said.

"Feeling good about it?" said Frisk, looking, if anything, a little nervous.

"I mean, it's a triple bypass, Frisk. Not like I haven't done enough of those in my lifetime. Imagine I'll be doing a fair few more if America's heart health gets any worse!"

I'd meant to make a joke, but my cavalier attitude seemed to make Frisk flinch. "Okay," he said a little defensively. "I'll be seeing you." I watched him walk away, clipboard in hand. Had I done something to offend someone?

About an hour later, I had a call from Zoe's mom, Megan.

"Adrian," she said languidly, sounding as though she'd been trapped in yet another interminably boring meeting. "Mind if I come down in five minutes to have a talk with you?"

"Sure thing," I said. I was busy typing up some of my notes from last week while a half-eaten sandwich sat on my desk next to a cup of coffee from the secret espresso machine.

In a little while, Megan came in. "Afternoon, Megan," I said. "To what do I owe the pleasure? Anything you need help with?"

Megan Hollis looked at me severely. I'd never seen her look so severe in her life. There was nothing wrong with it—Megan was an intelligent, confident woman, after all. But the look in her eyes said something more. It was almost as if...

"How are you feeling, Adrian?" she said, sitting down. "I realize jumping into a senior position like this can be fairly difficult, especially during the first few weeks."

Again, I bristled at that remark. I felt like people were dancing around me today. It was a feeling I hated and one which made me want to knit my brows together and get angry. But I chided myself at the thought. *Fuoco*, I said to myself again and put on as much of a smile as I could muster.

"I'm doing fine, Megan," I said. "You and Frisk both seem a little worried about me today."

Megan seemed a little startled. "So, you've spoken to Dr. Frisk?" she said.

I looked back at her. "Not really," I said. "He's asked me to have a chat with him this morning. Why?"

Megan looked at me. Then, slowly, a thin smile spread across her face. It was the smile someone gives when they know they've caught you in a lie, and your excuses are too ridiculous for even you to go on making them. Only, I was struggling to figure out exactly what it was I was supposed to be making excuses *for*.

"Are you feeling okay about your surgeries today? You know, if there's a problem with the supply box, the cabinet, or anything, you can talk to Frisk. Or to me, if you feel more comfortable."

I looked at her. There seemed to be a mixture of concern and contempt on her face. Those weren't expressions I was used to seeing from people.

"I'll let you know if I have any concerns, Megan. I have none at all."

"I should hope not," Megan said, practically under her breath. I didn't like her tone at all, but I didn't want to say anything about it.

"I have surgery in fifteen minutes," I said. "If you don't mind..."

"All right, Adrian," she said. "Well, if there's anything you need, let me know."

"Thanks," I said. "Will do."

Is it just my imagination, or is everyone acting crazy today?

*

The surgery went well—it went perfectly, in fact. After I'd removed my scrubs and washed myself, I jogged back upstairs to the wards. Finally, I got to Frisk's office and knocked on the door.

"Frisk?" I said casually. "You in here, pal?"

He looked up from his desk, and I saw a dark expression cross his eye. "Ah," he said. "Please, come in, Adrian."

I sat down. Frisk crossed his legs and took off his spectacles. I noticed he was tapping them lightly on his knee. It was something he did when he was nervous. Like, when he had something to hide.

"Adrian," he said, "I must admit, it's just...well, it's terrific having a doctor of your capabilities around here. It's really improved the place. Someone of your character, well. Let's just say..." he said, heaving himself forward, and resting an elbow on his knee while he fidgeted with the glasses, "...that I'm delighted you're here."

"Thanks," I said nervously. "I must admit, this sounds like a prelude to something."

"Well, it is," he said. "I don't know what it's like at Johns Hopkins or what the...uh...culture is, but, well, Chelsey showed me the email you sent to her last night, and I just thought it was appropriate to say..."

"Email?" I said.

"...That we don't really take well to that kind of language around here," said Frisk. "Now, I know you're a forceful character.

And I understand more than anyone the stresses of the job. But that doesn't give you the right to—"

"Hang on, hang on a minute," I said. I fixed him with a gaze. "Frisk, I didn't email Chelsey anything last night. Why would I be emailing the head nurse on the ward on a Sunday night? Anything I had to say to her, I could have said this morning."

Frisk looked at me. He narrowed his eyes as though this somehow made everything worse.

"You're saying," he mused, "that you didn't email Chelsey last night?"

"No," I said. "Of course not. Why would I do that when there was nothing urgent?"

Frisk reached over and took his computer monitor. He still used the old-style computer with a monitor and an enormous CPU attached to it.

"Adrian," he said, "Chelsey forwarded it to me. It's from you."

I looked at the email on the screen.

From: chelsey10@canonhospitalpersonnel.us

To: dfrisk@canonhospitalpersonnel.us

Date: 07/20/2023 00:16

Subject: Fw: Fucking Catastrophe

Chelsey,

I don't know what kind of fucking show you think you're running here, but sort the goddamned supply cabinet and sterilization boxes out. They're a maximum fucking catastrophe. You fucking pricks get your act together before I come over there and whip your asses.

A.

I peered at the email. "This was sent from...me? From my account."

"I'm glad," Frisk said diplomatically, "that in the clear light of day, you're as shocked as I am. You're new in this career, Adrian, and we don't want to make a big fuss. But you can't go around talking to people like this."

"I...But, I didn't," I said. "I mean, I wouldn't. I didn't send this email."

Frisk looked at me. I realized the look in his eye was sympathy. He thought I'd made a social blunder by sending an explicit email to a colleague and was trying to cover it up!

"Wait a minute," I said, standing up. "Wait a minute."

"Adrian," Frisk said, a little disappointed.

But I was gone.

I went down the room to my office and opened up my emails. I looked in the **Sent** folder. There it was.

I was shocked. It was the same email that I'd seen in Frisk's office. Someone had either logged onto my computer or hacked the email server in order to send it. I looked through the Sent folder and then found another email sent at the same time last night.

From: alawson@canonhospitalpersonnel.us

To: mhollis@canonhospitalpersonnel.us

Date: 07/20/2023 00:17

Subject: This Place Sucks

Megan,

We are going to need to have a SERIOUS talk tomorrow about the way things are run here. Staff work like pigs. It's disgusting.

A.

I looked at the email. They were sent from my account. My password was a goddamn ISBN book number. There was no way someone could have guessed it. The system had been hacked, for sure. Someone was trying to make me out to be an asshole.

"No one tries to make me look like an asshole," I muttered. "I'm the only one who gets to be an asshole in my life."

I got up and left. I left a voicemail for the medical secretary. "Cancel my afternoon appointments, please." I needed time to clear my head. And to figure out who was doing this to me.

Chapter 17

Zoe

I came home from my shift on Tuesday morning and slept. I was due back in at 8 am the following morning, but by the time I woke up, it was almost dark. I couldn't believe I'd slept for such a long time, and I decided to get some fresh air.

I stepped out of the front door onto my porch in a pair of shorts and my pajama shirt. I was wary of Wesley's presence in the house next to me.

I'd managed to avoid Adrian so far, scheduling in night shifts where he had day shifts, and working doubles when he had singles. I didn't want to see him right now. I was too confused, and my head was a mess. His reaction had been unprovoked, sure, but now I began to think that *I* was the one going mad. What had Wesley meant when he spoke to me in the kitchen? He seemed so out of character and strange. It was unnerving.

I looked towards Giulia's house and saw the porch light was on. *Thank God for small mercies!*

I put on some flip-flops and headed over.

Ever since we'd moved in on the same block, Giulia and I had established a code. Giulia had named it 'The Twinkle Code,' a name I wholeheartedly disagreed with because it seemed like something a fourteen-year-old would come up with. It meant you left your porchlight on if you wanted to talk or if you needed to hear someone speak to you.

I knocked on her front door. Giulia appeared behind the screen and opened it with one deft movement. "You came," she said drily, holding a wine glass in her hand.

Inside, we sat on the sofa. But rather than spilling her heart out to me immediately, Giulia was quiet. I didn't like that one bit.

"Giulia..." I said, "...ever since I met you, you've never stopped talking to me. So, right now, you're scaring me."

"I'm scared," said Giulia. "Well, not scared. Spooked, I guess."

"What happened?"

"Well, yesterday afternoon, I came home from work, and this really funny thing happened...or at least, I think it happened."

"Oh yeah?"

"I found a cat in my house."

I blinked and paused. "Giulia."

"What?"

"That's it? There was a cat in your house?"

"No, silly! That's like, part one of the mystery."

"Oh. Sorry. Go on."

"Anyway, I shooed it out...but then I thought, 'How did it get here?' So I looked all over for some kind of hole in the ceiling or the floor or whatever. But I couldn't find it. But the back door wasn't locked."

"Maybe you forgot to lock it, opened it one morning, and the cat came in?"

"But I didn't. I didn't open it yesterday. After what happened with Adrian's car, I triple check my locks every day."

"Hm. Okay. So what's part two?"

Giulia sighed a little and got a little more comfy, flopping around on the sofa while she rearranged a few of her cushions.

"Wesley was in the house this afternoon."

"What?" I said quietly.

"He was in here."

I felt my shoulders tense up and a slow, creeping fear moved up my spine.

"What do you mean he was here?"

"Well, you know how I'm always late on Tuesdays because of the gym? Well, today I didn't go. Instead, I just stayed late for half an hour grading papers. So, I got back an hour earlier. And when I came in, I found Wesley in my kitchen."

"That's weird."

"You're telling me it's weird! I asked him what he was doing there, and he kind of looked around. His face went all red, and then," Giulia said, "he told me he'd come over asking to borrow something, and the back door was unlocked, so he'd let himself in, and that's when I came home."

I frowned. I believed Giulia's story, for sure. That did sound like the kind of creepy thing Wesley would be up to. But I was still trying to hold on to the idea that Wes might be strange rather than dangerous—even if his personality change in my kitchen had utterly stunned me.

"Is there any chance he was telling the truth?"

"No, baby, and I'm telling you why. Because the back door was locked. I checked it this morning. Twice."

I didn't say anything, but Giulia finished the thought for herself.

"No doubt about it. He picked the lock."

"Do you wanna talk to the police?"

"The police?" Giulia scoffed. "Like they'd help. They won't even admit that Adrian's house got broken into or that someone got in here and scratched his car. They just refused to investigate the incidents. Even though he says he saw someone on the property a few nights before."

"That's awful. I wish I could do something to help you guys." A few days ago, Giulia had dropped by to tell me about what happened at Adrian's house, and I hated to pretend I knew nothing about it.

"Well, you could talk to Adrian for me. You know, since you guys seem to be getting along a bit better these days. And you see more of him than me too! It's like he's been avoiding me or something. He always used to do that when we were younger, you know, when he had a girlfriend or something."

I felt a tinge of color blush on my cheek. I felt guilty about not being able to tell Giulia. But even if I was her best friend, my feelings for Adrian were strong. Being apart for a few days under such strained circumstances had only made me think of him more and want him more. I was too deeply involved with him now for confessing to Giulia to be a simple matter. Even if I didn't think it would hurt our friendship, it was inevitable now. She'd feel betrayed that we'd kept the secret from her.

I leaned back on the sofa and then reached for the glass of wine Giulia had poured for me. Taking a sip, a thought flashed through my mind.

"Hey, Giulia," I said a little nervously.

She looked at me. "What, Zoe?"

"Does...does Wesley speak Italian? I mean, have you ever heard him..."

Giulia looked at me. She gave an odd, half-smile.

"No. Why. Have you?"

"Yeah?"

Giulia frowned. "It makes sense since he is *Italian*," she said. "I guess that's partly why I liked the look of him," she said a little bashfully. "He looks like...I mean, I guess his face...it's how I imagine my dad would look."

I nodded. "He looks pretty similar to Adrian, doesn't he?" I sprang from my position. "Let's change the subject. Tell me about work. Any more drama with the coach..."

Giulia's eyes lit up, a bit of the glum draining away. "You will not believe what he did today. So..."

After we'd talked for a little bit about some nicer things, I went back to my house and made dinner. I hoped I'd done a good job cheering Giulia up. Somehow, it would compensate for my awful job cheering up Adrian.

Later that night, I checked my emails before going to work and saw a strange one. It was a message from Dr. Frisk, asking if any of the nurses felt they'd been the target of an unfair or aggressive email from a senior doctor. I frowned. If Frisk had sent it to the cardiology ward, there was only one senior doctor who'd have sent anything, and that was Adrian.

I took out my phone and checked the work group chat. I tried to stay off it on my days off, except for the occasional emoji in solidarity with a particularly gruesome message. I scrolled through the messages, which were all reacting with laughter and outrage to something.

can't believe he'd send that

what a jerk!!!

Lol xxx let us clean that up for u hon

Finally, I scrolled up and found what had prompted my co-workers' strong feelings. It was a screenshot of an email. A horrible email, filled with cursing and a threatening tone—the kind of email you'd write if you were drunk.

The email was addressed from Adrian.

I sat down, overwhelmed at the thought of it. I read the thing again. It was disgusting—not because it really said anything crazy, but because it was so...

Hateful.

I couldn't believe Adrian had actually sent that to someone. My first thought was that he'd been drinking. But then, I struggled to remember a time when I'd seen him drink more than two glasses of wine. Adrian looked after his body so much I couldn't believe he'd actually get hammered, especially not on his own, in his house.

So why had he said such mean things?

I knew something about him that no one else did right now. I knew about the break-in and the toll it had taken on him. And wasn't something up with his business in New York and his investments? If everything was going wrong at the same time, could it push him to speak to someone that way?

I sighed because there was an alternative truth I was avoiding.

Maybe Adrian was just like that. Maybe the kind of person who could amass his wealth and power and had the drive to study to be a doctor was the kind of person who went over the line.

I didn't notice, and slowly, as the shadows grew and night fell, I realized I'd been struck by the email and had been reading it for hours.

Then, I heard a noise in the distance, like the slamming of a door.

I stood up. The noise had come from Wesley's house.

I went over to the window on the far side of my living room, which had a view of Wesley's driveway, though not his front porch. I didn't want to expose myself to him on the front porch if he was out there.

Wesley was walking down the steps of his porch now. In his hand, he was carrying something enormous.

I recognized what it was from a time I'd had to go to the hospital basement. It was a floodlight—an enormous bulb designed for illuminating a parking lot or a building with no power.

I watched Wesley get back and ducked down, hiding behind my windowsill. Then, slowly, I looked to see if he was there.

I waited, and then, finally, I heard him come out again. He was coming down the steps with a pair of extension cables, the kind that you can wrap around a wheel that sits on the ground.

He got into his car and drove away. I checked the clock. It was 11:04 pm.

"Software engineer, my ass," I muttered as his car sped away into the night.

Chapter 18

Adrian

"I just wanna talk to him!"

"Sir, Detective Vance isn't available to speak to you right now, but—"

"Let me SEE HIM!" I said, pounding my fist on the desk.

There was a moment of quiet in the otherwise busy police precinct. I took my hand off the desk and looked around. Two teenagers in the corner who'd been brought in for getting their hands on some fireworks hissed and giggled a little bit. Their mother shot them a warning look, then looked at me.

I could see what she was thinking in her eyes. *Crazy.*

"There's no need to be like that, sir," said the woman at the desk, coolly. "And I suggest you watch your manners from now on."

"I'm sorry, I'm just...it's so frustrating. I've asked to make a complaint. I know Detective Vance is handling my existing complaints. I want to speak to him."

"You'll have to make an appointment," said the officer at the desk, turning back to look at her computer screen.

"But that doesn't make sense," I protested. "Someone is personally trying to harass me, to get at me. Vance knows this. I've spoken to him about it before. He keeps blowing me off."

"Not surprised about that," muttered another officer behind the desk. He gave me a sympathetic look before his colleague turned around to deliver a withering glance.

"You got something better to do than stand behind me all day, Parker?"

"Sorry. Yes, ma'am." The officer scuttled away.

The police officer turned around and looked at me. "Sir, I will relay your complaints to Detective Vance, and he will contact you when he can. In the meantime, go home. You're obviously a little excited."

"It's not good enough..." I shook my head. "...just not good enough." I felt my fist clenching. "Not good enough," I said, a little louder, and turned to my left.

I marched down the corridor. "SIR!" called the officer on the desk. "Where do you think you're going?"

"Doesn't wanna speak to me?" I said to myself. "Well, I'll speak to him."

I turned the handle of Vance's office and threw open the door. The detective sat up from something on his desk, which he quickly put away into the drawer.

"Dr. Lawson?" said the detective. "Just what do you think you're doing in my office? This is a police station, not a..."

"Can it, Vance," I said, holding up a hand. The detective stopped talking.

"So far..." I said, "...in the last month, my sister's house may have been broken into, my car's been vandalized, I've given an eyewitness account of an intruder on my property, someone rammed my door in, and I've now got emails in my Sent box that I never sent," I said breathlessly. "I want to know what you're going to do about it."

Vance chuckled. "Emails in your sent box? Wish I had some of those."

That made me lose my temper. I turned around, and as I did, I kicked a trashcan sitting on the ground. Its contents spilled open.

"Hey now," said Vance, "that's *enough*."

He stood, and his hand moved down. It was an almost imperceptible gesture, but I knew what it meant.

Vance was moving his hand closer to his waist, where his gun was holstered.

"I understand you're under a lot of pressure," he snarled, "but you do not get to come in here and tell me how to do my job. Particularly after you've been belligerent and rude to my staff."

Two officers from the Cañon City Police Department had caught up to me. One of them clapped a hand on my shoulder.

"Now," said Vance, sneering, "the next time I see you in here, Adrian, I'm going to arrest you. Got it? Any more complaints or comments you have," he said, sitting down, "can be forwarded to my office by email."

The officers were pushing me out.

"As long as, of course," Vance crooned, "you use polite language. No curse words."

The police officers had pushed me out onto the sidewalk. As I stood there in the heat of the afternoon sun, I watched in the distance as a stray breeze stirred up some dust.

Then, I realized something.

How did Vance know the emails had curse words?

*

The following day, I went back into the office. Zoe had left before I'd arrived, which frustrated me to no end. I needed to see her. But first, I had something else to do.

Chelsey was working at the front desk. I saw her as I was coming down the corridor and thought I saw her raise an eyebrow.

"Can I speak to you?"

Chelsey shrugged and stood up. She wasn't looking me in the eye. Clearly, she didn't want to give me the satisfaction. In the breakroom, I spoke to her.

"I'm really sorry you got that in your inbox. But I didn't send it."

Chesley made a face and sighed. "Oh, brother. You know, Doctor, you didn't have to apologize," she said, walking away. "But don't *lie*."

I screwed up my face and smoothed it out with my hands, leaning against the wall. It's true what they say. Everybody's ready to believe the worst.

I was running out of options.

I still had one, though. And I'd already called it in before I worked through the day. I'd asked Charlie to find me a private detective. Someone discreet, and talented.

Around 6 pm I got a text from him. It simply said, "I'm here."

I texted back the code for the employee parking lot and stood. I slipped out of my office and passed the front desk. "I'm stepping out for a second."

"Must be nice," one of the nurses on the desk muttered as I left the ward and made my way down to the parking lot.

There, I searched up and down the rows of cars until one flashed its headlights. I walked over, without even batting an eyelid. To anyone watching from a hospital window or a passerby, it would look completely casual, like I was walking to my own car.

I got in and sat in the passenger seat. Next to me was a man. And there wasn't a lot more I could say about him.

I was impressed by just how, well, ordinary he looked. He was in his late twenties, a little thin, but not so thin you'd remember him. His jaw was coated in rough stubble, and he wore a gray t-shirt and a blazer.

"Duncan Reed, private investigator. I don't think we need to go into it any more than that. You're Adrian Lawson. I'm going to pretend I haven't seen your name on the news. What can I help you with?"

"It's a couple of things."

"A couple of things means a couple of jobs. A couple of tails. That costs extra."

"I want to make it clear that money is no object. But I also like to know exactly what it is I'm getting for my money."

"Don't worry. You'll get it. I'm particularly thorough with record-keeping, bills, and so on."

"Describe to me your usual clientele."

He smirked. "There is no 'usual,'" he explained. "Infidelity covers a lot of it, sure. But there's more business than you would think. People stealing secrets from each other. Insider trading. That kind of thing."

"Ever follow any police officers?" I said quietly.

Reed paused for a moment, then continued in the same dull monotone in which he'd been speaking before. "As I said, it's really a question of expense."

"What's your rate?"

"Hundred-and-forty per hour. Plus expenses for gas, travel, etc. Do you want pictures?"

"They'd be helpful, yes."

"So, who are we looking at?"

"Detective Vance. There's something up with him. He isn't taking my case seriously...I don't know if someone paid him off or something. I'm 100% sure he may be in league with someone who's trying to wreck my life. This person is responsible for burgling—or trying to burgle—my house. They're also responsible for hacking into my email account at work."

"What did they take from the burglary?"

"Nothing," I said. "But they were looking for something. Something they believe that I have."

The detective nodded. "Anything else?"

"Yeah," I said. "If possible, I want you to find out about someone for me. Someone who's dead. I'd like to know where she came from and why they emigrated her to the United States."

"Right," said the detective. "Name?"

"Estella Lawson. My mother."

*

The last time I'd seen my mother had been two years ago. It was at a barbeque she was hosting in her backyard. My mother was a wonderful cook, and I'd been helping her at the grill, turning steaks and peppers on the hot, charcoal fire when she chided me in that gentle way she always did.

"Adriano," she said softly. "*Isn't this nice? Being here with your sister, with your family? With cara Zoe?*"

"Yes, mama," I smiled. I knew what was coming. The inevitable lecture. Beyond us, over the other side of the garden, I could see the neighbors sitting under the shade.

"*Much better than being in New York. You're not going to stay there forever, are you?*"

"I don't know," I said. "*I'm enjoying working at the hospital. And the business...*"

"*Business, business, business,*" she tutted. "*That's all it ever is with you. I don't like it. Why do you have to be in these magazines and things.*" She wasn't angry. If anything, she sounded worried about me.

I sighed. "*Nothing wrong with wanting to make my mark on the world,*" I said. "*You told me that.*"

"*I did,*" she said, and then it seemed like she was going to say more. Perhaps she did. But I was too busy looking at Zoe, who'd just appeared.

She'd brought her boyfriend: some dull guy who worked near Cañon. Chris, or maybe Kyle, was his name. Zoe was awkwardly introducing Kyle to Giulia. He looked bored and a little uncomfortable in his smart shirt and pants. I didn't like the look of him at all.

149

"*Zoe's brought a friend,*" said my mother, slyly.

"*Yeah,*" I said.

"*Why don't you go and say hello?*" she said. "*I can run my own kitchen.*"

"*I want to help you,*" I protested with a small laugh. But inside, the truth was that I was boiling. Zoe could do so much better than this guy, who didn't even seem interested in talking to her friends, parents, or family.

The truth was that I missed my mother and Giulia, but I missed Zoe just as much. Sometimes she was all I thought about in New York.

After that fateful day about my mother's funeral, she was all I could think about, period.

So the following morning after speaking to the PI, I called Zoe. It rang for a bit, and I wondered if it would go to voicemail like the others when she answered.

"Hello?" It was so good to hear her voice.

"Hi."

"Hi."

There was a pause. Neither of us knew what to say to each other. So I decided to say what was in my heart.

"I'm so sorry for the way I treated you over the weekend. I was upset, and angry. And I let my feelings drive you away. I didn't want that."

I heard Zoe burst into her characteristically happy stream-of-consciousness.

"Oh, it's okay! Besides, I was probably overreacting. And, on the plus side—"

"Zoe. It's not okay."

"Oh."

"You didn't deserve to be spoken to like that."

"Well," said Zoe. "Don't do it again, I guess."

"Noted. Can I take you out tonight?"

There was a pause on the phone. I winced. Was she about to reject me?

"I'll let you take me out..." said Zoe, "...but there's something we need to talk about."

"What?"

"Adrian, did you really send those horrible emails?"

Chapter 19

Zoe

I knew just from how Adrian spoke on the phone that he was having a rough day. I could hear the strain in his voice, and part of it made me feel even more strongly about him. He was suffering under so many pressures and had so much to deal with. And yet, even in all of that, he'd still called me and apologized. He'd made it clear I didn't have to make an excuse for him, that he was accountable for his behavior, and it was one of the most attractive things I'd learned about him yet.

But there was still one matter to deal with: the way that Adrian had written to Chelsey. So, after I'd finished my shift, he picked me up. We decided to take a walk before dinner. I had nothing special to wear, but Adrian told me it didn't matter.

"You look amazing, just the way you are," he said as we made our way down the streets. I loved this time of day when the sun was beginning to set and shops were closing. It was like the city took on a completely new characteristic.

"Thanks." I smiled, looking down. I never knew how to deal with it when he complimented me like that. But I held true to my purpose, even though being with such a gorgeous, intelligent guy made my heart spin and my head cloud.

"Adrian," I said, "I thought...when I read those emails..."

He didn't say anything, but let me finish. I glanced over to him and saw his eyes burning and his usual sullen expression descend.

"I didn't think you could have written it."

He looked up, his face clearing a little. "Really?" he said. "Why did you think that?"

I thought about it for a moment as we turned a corner in the city and passed a bookshop. Inside, I could see the walls lined with stories. Stories we tell ourselves about where we're from and who we are.

"I thought," I said, "that it was out of character for you. That you'd never—that you probably would never—do something like that."

I stopped on the corner. Ahead of us, to the West, the sun had sunk low in the sky, casting long shadows behind us. But through the gaps in the buildings, it was blazing, strong as ever, too bright to look at.

"I want to believe that's true," I said. "And I think you're going to tell me it is."

"But, you don't know if when I tell you, I'll tell you what you need to hear or want to hear."

"So, what I was going to say is, don't worry about telling me what I want to hear or what I need to hear. Just tell me the truth."

His eyes met mine for a moment; then he looked away.

"Adrian, who sent those emails?"

He looked at me.

"I don't know." I let out a breath. It wasn't a sigh. More of a gasp. Barely quiet enough to hear. "But it wasn't me."

I searched his face. He was telling the truth. Adrian had a few telltale signs when he was lying, and knowing him so long, I could usually suss out whether he was not telling the truth. His deep brown eyes in the dying sunlight begged me to believe him.

We passed a side street, one which led down the side of the stores to white picket fences and back gardens beyond. I put a hand on one of Adrian's strong, muscular shoulders.

"Come here," I said.

"What?" he replied absentmindedly.

I pulled him into the alley and looked up at his face, dark eyes, and thick, dark hair. I wanted him to know that I was going to stand by him, whatever happened.

And the only way I could think to show it was by reaching up, putting my hand to his cheek, and kissing him, gently and tenderly.

He kissed me back, and I felt my hunger and need for his body blossom inside of me. My want for Adrian could shake me to my core at the best of times, but now, I felt it most of all in his time of need.

I let myself down, back off the tips of my toes, and I could see him smiling at me. The effect was tangible. I could feel it in his body, as he relaxed with himself for a moment. A few lines of worry had disappeared from around his eyes.

I took his hand in mine and squeezed it. "Let's go eat."

We headed to *The Bistro*. It was by far the nicest place in town, though it wasn't as stuffy as the place at the hotel. *The Bistro* made food that you actually wanted to eat.

As we sat down, I eyed Adrian's shoulders, his torso. He looked somehow a little worn.

"When was the last time you ate something?"

Adrian looked confused. "I...I don't know. Yesterday morning, maybe?"

I opened my mouth. "Adrian. It's evening right now. You're telling me you haven't had anything to eat for thirty-six hours?"

He laughed, but it wasn't funny. I was beginning to get seriously worried about him. And while I wanted to relax and enjoy our date, I couldn't help but continue to ask him about the mysterious person who Adrian thought was behind all of it.

"Nothing is normal right now," I spoke a little glumly. "First, there's Wesley. You know he was in Giulia's house the other day? Like, while she was out?"

Adrian grimaced. I knew he didn't like Wesley, and to some extent, he was kind of smug about being proved right. "I took that guy for a creep the moment I saw him," he muttered.

"It gets worse," I said. "I saw him leaving his house last night with...get this. Floodlights?"

"That's kinda strange. Does he have, like, a night job?"

"No! He mostly works from home or out of this weird corporate office block on the other side of town, or so he says."

"You know something kind of odd about him? He looks like..."

Adrian searched for the words.

"...like he's related to you."

"Yeah. Exactly. I mean, that's exactly what I was going to say. How did you know?"

"Aside from the fact it's obvious? Giulia said the same thing."

It was becoming clear to us that something strange was happening, but I didn't really know what. After our food arrived, Adrian tried to get me to talk about something else.

"Anyway, I wanted to focus on you, Zoe."

"Me? What is there to talk about?"

"I don't know. I guess I'm just interested in who you are. Pretend we don't know each other. What would you tell me?"

"Okay." I paused and tried to think, then giggled. "I can't think of anything. I'm really not that interesting."

"Yes, you are! Come on, you've gotta tell me something about you. Something you've never told anyone else."

"Okay. I tell people I don't like Disney adults..."

"But..."

"But, secretly, my favorite film ever is that silly cartoon where Mickey, Goofy, and Donald go up the hill in the RV or the trailer or whatever."

"*Mickey's Trailer*. Love it. Great cartoon."

"WHAT?"

Adrian Lawson, the brooding handsome billionaire doctor, likes...Mickey Mouse?

"I mean, I haven't seen it since I was, like, twelve..." laughed Adrian, "...but yeah. You know that was made in 1938."

"You say you haven't seen it since you were twelve," I said suspiciously, "but you know the year they made it and everything."

"Oh, I know all those. I've got, like, a photographic memory for films. Try me."

"Okay. What year did *Titanic* come out."

"Too easy. 1997."

"The Poseidon Adventure?"

"Wow, we're really stuck with the sinking ship theme, aren't we? 1972."

"Damn. Those are like the only two I know without looking it up. That's crazy."

We were laughing and joking, just like old times.

"So, come on. We know your favorite film. What else would you tell me if this was our first date?"

"Well, first things first, I'd tell you that my mom ran the hospital, and my dad was the district judge. So, if you want to stay healthy and on the right side of the law..." I said, chuckling, "...you'd better make sure I get home on time."

Adrian sighed. "You know, one of those emails got sent to your mom. I still haven't had the chance to explain. Or apologize."

"You don't need to apologize," I said, shrugging my shoulders. "My mom's..."

"What?" asked Adrian, because I'd trailed off into silence.

"Because my mom is..." I said, staring toward the back of the restaurant.

"Your mom's what? What is it, Zoe?"

"My mom's coming this way," I said.

My mom, Megan, had arrived at our table within a minute.

"Mrs. Hollis," Adrian said. He wiped his hands and mouth, stood, and lightly shook her hand. Megan looked at his hand, like it was a dirty napkin he'd just placed in her palm.

"Good evening, Adrian," my mom said, her voice cold. She turned to me, pretending she'd just noticed me sitting at the table.

"Good evening, Zoe!" she said cheerily and politely. I knew that smile. That smile meant: *I can't begin to explain how much you've embarrassed me.*

"Hi, Mom," I said, shifting awkwardly in my chair.

"I have to say, Adrian, I had no idea you took your nurses out for dinner at *The Bistro*," my mom said breezily, looking around her.

"Zoe works hard, and she deserves a treat," said Adrian. "I wanted to talk to her for a while. Isn't that right, Zoe?"

He looked at me, and I looked at my mom. I nodded. "Yeah," I said. "Mom, we've had this planned for weeks. It just kept getting put off."

"I mean, I know you two grew up together..." said my mom, "...but perhaps you should be a little more careful. It can lead to consequences that neither of you want..."

My ears stung like they did that time I forgot to do my homework in fourth grade.

"Still, I'm sure little worries about professionalism and conduct don't affect you, do they, Adrian?" said my mother. "Especially given that we have more pressing matters to worry about. Staff working like pigs, for example."

"Megan," began Adrian. "I am deeply sorry..."

"I have to get back to your father," she said. "Have a nice evening, Zoe. And you too, Adrian."

She stalked away, and Adrian sat down.

"Well, at least you've been introduced to my parents now," I said, trying to lighten the mood.

"My Italian ancestors would be delighted," Adrian said, staring at a stray breadcrumb on the tablecloth.

*

The romantic mood at *The Bistro* had been killed slightly by the surprise arrival of my mom, so we didn't stay for dessert. But I still didn't want to leave Adrian. With the world falling apart, he was a comfort to me, and by the bridge over the river in town, I stood close to him, leaning on his broad chest.

"I'm sorry about my mom," I said. "It's just..."

"I understand," said Adrian. "You don't have to justify anything to me."

I turned to him. In the near-darkness, I could still see glimmers of light in Adrian's dark, brown eyes. I reached up to him and kissed his mouth, and he kissed me back, slow, and deep, and strong.

"I think we've earned some time to ourselves," he whispered. "Away from everyone else."

Back at Adrian's house, he let me in. Slipping off his shoes, Adrian went to the cabinet and made us a pair of Old-Fashioneds'. "Come on," he said, slyly. "You haven't even seen the rest of my castle."

I smiled and followed him up the stairs, which were covered in plush, red carpet. On the top landing, I looked out through the stone arched windows into Adrian's garden below. He led me along the landing to a dark, wooden door, which opened into his room.

It was beautiful. Adrian's bed was enormous, covered in soft, satin sheets. Around the room were pieces of period furniture.

I took a sip of my drink and put it down on the bedside table.

Adrian was standing by the window.

"I always wanted a place like this," he said. "But it never made sense until you stepped into it."

I put my arms around him and rested my head on his back, but Adrian turned. He knew what he wanted. And I wanted it too.

Kissing me, I felt one of his arms reach down and close around my waist. There was no escape, just surrender to the gentle movements of his hand on my cheek, his mouth as it traced a slow curve towards my neck. And again, the impossible feeling of being one with the man I cared for most in the world overtook me.

I let my hands reach for him, and they untucked his shirt from his dress pants and reached beneath the soft flesh and hard muscle around his abdomen. I pressed my palms up against him, warming myself from his heat and his lust, and let my nails catch on his back as I did.

Adrian growled appreciatively and stepped towards me. I stepped back. I felt like a wild animal cornered me, and the feeling was fantastic.

Before I knew it, I'd been pushed backward. Not that it hurt, because the bed was soft, inviting, and within moments Adrian, free of his blazer, was on top of me, safety and calm descending as he began to show me I belonged to him. Slowly, his kisses turned a little feral, and I felt him delicately issuing love bites over my neck, where dark, purple roses would spring the following morning.

"Adrian," I said breathlessly, but he barely heeded me, pulling my dress up and over my head until I lay before him, exposed.

He kissed furiously now, showering my entire body with praise as his mouth made its way down my chest and to my stomach. I stopped, shivering with delight, anticipating another taste of his mouth. But Adrian had other ideas.

Slowly, he bent over me, kissing my chest while his hand slipped below the hem of my panties. I became aware of his middle and ring fingers pressing gently on my clit, and swooned, sighing and moaning with a high-pitched whine that only made him more excited.

Adrian began to finger me gently, moving in little circles. Then, slowly, he dropped to his knees and pulled my panties down until I was completely naked for him.

With his left hand, he carried on stimulating my clit, while I felt his right hand exploring the lips of my pussy. I shuddered as he touched me, knowing what he wanted, overwhelmed and excited and nervous and confident, all at once. I surrendered to his touch. I was his woman. He could do with me what he pleased.

Adrian entered me, first with his middle finger, then with his ring finger too. It was blissful. He pushed inside of me, little by little. Then, I looked down and saw him give me a wicked smile as his middle finger curled upwards. He began to move in time with his other hand.

Oh, I see, I thought, and even my thoughts were breathless. *I finally see. He's got me right where he wants me. I'm his. All his.* And while I thought these things, enormous waves of pleasure began to stretch down my legs and up my waist, as Adrian fingered me to a roiling, shaking climax that sent my head spinning and made me scream his name to the top of the roof.

When I was finished, when I'd stopped shaking, he eased out of me, and bent down to kiss me between my legs a little while. It was delightful, if sensitive, but I still wanted more somehow—with this man and this man alone. I wasn't done.

I pulled him towards me, and he eased himself up. I could feel just by how it fell against my thigh that my orgasm had caused him to acquire an enormous, throbbing erection.

"Now..." I whispered, smiling and stroking the light stubble that had grown on his face, "...fuck me."

Easing himself inside was easy, even for a man of Adrian's size, because I was so wet from the climax I'd just had. Overcome with desire, I wrapped my legs around him, ignoring the dull ache in my muscles from the shock they'd just experienced.

He showed me no mercy, thrusting hard, even as I moaned and writhed beneath him. When I tried to soothe his furious passion, he raised both my arms above my head, pinning me down by my wrists on the bed. God, I loved it when he did that!

Adrian fucked me, roughly, but sensually, and as we settled into a nice, steady rhythm together, I felt myself enjoying the experience more than I ever had.

"Let me go on top," someone whispered. It was me, but a part of me I'd never heard speak before. A part liberated by his heat, who could speak her desires.

I practically leaped up and put him on his back, where I could control his pleasure, tightening around his enormous dick so that I could more effectively make him cry and groan with satisfaction. As I felt him beginning to come for me, I placed my hands on his chest, angling myself over Adrian so that I could see his expression, his open mouth and eyes tightly shut, half-pleasure, half-agony, as he gave it up for me, all of it, and pulsed suddenly, coming inside me while I laughed, shouted, with joy.

Afterward, I fell off him, utterly exhausted by the sheer madness of the sex we'd just shared.

"That was the best...thing...ever," I said, staring up at the ceiling.

"You're incredible," he sighed.

"No, you," I replied.

"I...I..." His voice trailed off. I thought he was going to say something else, but Adrian was closing his eyes. Spent, tired, and helpless, I rested my head against his shoulder and surrendered to the deep darkness of sleep.

Chapter 20

Adrian

The following day, after making Zoe breakfast and promising to see her after work, I headed to my office. I set about apologizing to the board of executives for the email I'd sent to Megan and Chelsey. I copied in the whole staff. It was better to pretend to be guilty for the time being. People in town were starting to think I was crazy, anyway, and I'd already done enough to damage my relationship with Megan and the nurses on my ward.

I did the rounds on the ward and had a minor exploratory surgery at 1 pm. It took a while to find out what we were looking for, though, and without knowing it, three hours had slipped by just like that. After I got out, I returned to my desk and took out my mobile phone. I immediately saw that I'd had at least three missed calls from Charlie.

I called him back. "What's up?"

"You're not gonna like this."

"I'm not liking much of anything that is happening at the moment." That wasn't entirely true, I thought, reflecting on the incredible night in bed Zoe and I had shared together. But that was hardly relevant to my business in New York.

"They've asked for a meeting."

"When?"

"Tomorrow morning."

"God dammit."

The IRS was coming in to speak to us. They had an obligation to investigate the complaints made against me by an anonymous source. And since no one had access to the entire sweep of the accounts' funds except me, I was the investigation's principal shareholder. I'd need to be present for the meeting.

"For the sake of getting this sorted out," I said testily, "I will get a plane to New York. But, Charlie..."

"Yeah?"

"Please. Tell me this is going to be over."

"It will be. Once the meeting goes well, the person who's complained against us will need to go to a higher authority. At that point, their identity will be made public."

"And at that point," I said, "they won't have a leg to stand on."

*

I asked for the jet prepped and standing by at 9.30 pm. Before I left the house, I called Zoe.

"Adrian? Where are you? I thought that..."

"Zoe, I have to go to New York for a few days. I've left instructions. Enough people owe me favors for covering their shifts and have agreed to step in until I'm back."

"Okay."

"I'm sorry, sweetheart. I don't want to go. But they need me to be there for the investigation."

There was a pause. For a moment, I thought Zoe was going to be angry. But the voice which I heard on the phone wasn't angry. It was resigned, and I cursed myself for the situation into which I'd been placed.

"I just think we should have talked about this—"

A beep cut out what Zoe was saying, and I looked at my phone. It was the PI.

"Sorry? Zoe, what were you saying?"

"I was saying that—"

This time, there was a text tone. I looked at the phone.

Got important info. Call me whenever.

"Zoe, I'm sorry. Someone else is calling me. I need to go."

"Adrian!"

"What?"

"You're...you're doing it again."

"What am I doing again? Sorry, Zoe, I need to go. I'm going to be late for the plane."

I called Duncan Reed, the PI. "I'm at my house. Come over. I need to drive to the airfield. My driver will bring you back."

*

"This is a hell of a thing," said the PI. "But I no longer think you're crazy."

166

"Well, that's a relief," I said. "Is that what you drove up here to tell me?"

We were speeding down the freeway in my Bentley. I wanted to get to the airport in time. I was sitting in the back while Chris, my driver, was upfront.

"I've got a couple of things," he told me. "Firstly, he's not who he says he is. There was no Detective Vance in Chicago up until four months ago. Then he appears on police records. Then, two weeks after Detective Vance started to exist, he applied for a job in Cañon."

"Right," I said. "He's someone who exists on paper, so this guy can come and work in the police department. That should be enough to go to the cops with, right?"

"Well, not the local cops," said Reed. "I mean, they think he's perfectly real. They'll dismiss your claim outright. But if you ask the Chicago police..."

"Then they can verify the information for me, and Cañon Department will have to cross-reference his application for the job. And his references."

"That's it. Now, I was wondering, how does a guy like Vance manage to get a whole bunch of fake references and identification to get into a police department?"

"The same way someone manages to send emails from my account. Hacking. Malware."

"Sure thing," said the PI. "Thing is, that can't be Vance."

"Why not?" I said.

"Vance is no hacker, believe me." Reed laughed. "Trust me. I watched him using a phone the other day. Guy doesn't even own a smartphone. And you'd need one these days. The computer infrastructure out here is awful. And your computer was hacked with a smartphone."

"Isn't that just more suspicious?" I said. "Surely he has one hidden away."

"No, he doesn't. And that makes sense from where I'm standing. It would just be another reason to know more about someone. What, with social media and all. He's off the grid for a reason. Doesn't own a personal computer. My guess is, whoever this guy really is, he probably used to be a cop. But he probably ain't one anymore."

"Okay," I said. "So, who did the hacking?"

"My bet?" said Reed, producing a photo from a manilla envelope. "This guy. Vance met him last night at midnight. Went home from his shift, took his car, and drove out into Rouse Park. Luckily, me and Mister Telephoto Lens were also out for a stroll that evening."

The photo he showed me was grainy, in black-and-white.

"I couldn't use color. Too dark. Luckily, I had some more sensitive film in my bag."

It showed Vance, with his back to the camera, with another guy standing by a car.

I recognized that car. It was the same one I'd seen driving away from my house when I saw the intruder!

"That's him!" I said. I peered closely at his face. "Wesley?" I said, confused, then looked closer.

No. That was just my imagination. The man in the photograph might bear a passing resemblance to Wesley. But he must have been thirty years older, at least. His face was creased with lines, and he had a scar on one cheek or some kind of keloid. The raised, shiny texture was obvious—indicative of a cut to the face.

I was sure I'd read about that somewhere. I couldn't remember where. Was it something to do with gangs? I racked my brain, but nothing clicked.

"This guy's probably your guy, then. Either way, I didn't get his license plate. They were edgy and nervous, and I was not getting close to a bent cop and a burglar. Sorry. That's above my pay grade. As for your mother, I don't have anything on her. She turns up in New York when you were about three years old. She worked for a jeweler on 59th Street for a while. Before that? Nothing. No trace of Estella Lawson arriving in the US."

"Don't worry, you've earned your money," I said. We were pulling into the airfield now. "I just wanted to know if you were interested in doubling your fee."

"Sure."

"Take two days," I said, "and find out everything you can about a guy called Wesley Banks. He's my sister's next-door neighbor."

And, I thought to myself, *he looks for all the world like he's related to the man in this photograph.*

The jet was taxiing onto the runway as we arrived. It slowed down, and the door opened. I shook hands with Duncan Reed and asked Chris to return him to the house.

I jogged towards the plane, and as I did, I called Zoe.

"Zoe?" I said.

"Adrian? It's late. I've got work tomorrow. What are you calling me for?"

"Listen, Zoe. I wanted to apologize for hanging up on you. I've got a lot going on right now and..."

"And you need some time to yourself, right?"

I was shocked. It wasn't like Zoe to be so sarcastic with me.

"Adrian," Zoe said, "I'm stuck in this with you. I don't know why, but now, I'm defending you to everyone. From doctors, from nurses, from my goddamn parents. Doesn't that mean anything to you..."

"It does," I said, carefully, "and I'm grateful."

"Then don't go to New York. Leave it for tomorrow. Come and talk to me. Show me that I matter."

"Sir!" called the flight attendant. "We're going to miss our flight path if we don't take off now."

I froze, not knowing what to do. Should I stay with the woman who meant the most to me? Or should I go and try to make things right? I couldn't decide what to choose between.

"It sounds like you've made your choice," said Zoe and hung up.

I hung my head, sighed, and stepped onto the plane.

Chapter 21

Zoe

I'd hoped that Adrian would be able to see my point of view. But the fact that he wasn't even willing to explain why he needed to be away had hurt my feelings and left me bruised for the second time since the break-in at his house.

I wanted to call him again now that he was in New York. But some part of me realized that if I called him, it would only be to tell him what I was beginning to fear already: that we weren't compatible and that the distance Adrian was putting between us was already eroding my faith in him. I still thought fondly about the night we'd spent together, the mind-blowingly good sex we'd had, and the way we'd laughed and joked.

But I wasn't sure it was going to work.

Over the next few days, while I worked my shifts, I fretted and worried. Wes kept coming and going at strange hours. I wasn't entirely convinced he was really living in the house. Part of me—a part that was packed to the brim with fear like water in a jug—suspected that there was only one reason Wesley had moved into the house between me and Giulia in the first place.

I tried to put that darkening suspicion out of my mind, but as the nights grew even hotter, and I was kept awake at night by the heat and the sounds of cicadas outside, I began to realize that something was wrong.

As usual, it was Giulia who came to the rescue. She had a telepathic sense for when I was feeling down, and by the time Saturday morning came around and I had a day off, I was pretty miserable. I was content to stay in bed all morning and do nothing with my day, but around 10 am, I heard the doorbell ring.

I leaned over and peered out of the oval window of my bedroom, which looked onto the street. I normally left the blinds closed, especially when I wanted to sleep, but last night, I'd gotten up to crack the window—it was so hot—and I left it open. I saw Giulia come down from the porch and cross my lawn, looking back at the house. She looked up the window and saw me, sleepy and bed-headed, waving down.

"You got *FIVE MINUTES!*" she said, in an ominous tone, and left the house. "We're going on a little beauty day," she explained to me once I'd gotten dressed and come downstairs.

"What for?" I said pessimistically. "Not like I've got anyone to be beautiful for."

"Girl," said Giulia, with all the seriousness of a doctor counseling her patient to quit smoking or get clean. "You. Gotta. Respect. Yourself. Where's that happy-go-lucky girl I know so well?"

Her personality was infectious, and even I couldn't help smiling. "You're right," I laughed. "You're so goddamn right."

Giulia had the works planned. First off, we began at the gym with what Giulia referred to as "cardio." This consisted of speedy walking on a treadmill, with regular juice breaks. After that, we hit the steam room, and I sighed, relaxing in my towel as the hot water evaporated up and around me, opening my pores. I felt like I was cleansing away all the bad feelings. But I couldn't help but compare the gym's steam room with the *banya* at the resort Adrian had taken me to, and inevitably, I felt sad. However, I perked up when we got to the nail salon. I went for a manicure.

"You been sticking your hand in bleach?" said the girl at the counter as she began filing at my nails for me. "Your skin's a little, well. Bleachy."

"Uh, yeah, I'm a nurse," I said. "So I guess I gotta put my hands in a lot of things!"

"Gross," said the girl. "I find touching people's hands is enough for me."

She leaned in conspiratorially.

"Ever touched a..." she said, raising an eyebrow at me. "You know."

"Only about a hundred!" I laughed cheerily. I don't know if she was concerned by the tone in which I responded or inspired with respect for my profession, but she bent down and didn't say much else to me for the rest of the conversation.

"Whaddya think of these babies?" said Giulia as we left. She pointed down at her toes, which were now a shade of bright blue.

"Oh, wow," I said, a little jealously. "That's awesome."

"You know, I find the colors give you something to look at in the shower," she said nonchalantly. Grabbing my hand, she led me down the street. "It's iced-coffee hour," she said.

*

By the time we got back home, I was at once incredibly happy and slightly tired. I'd already tried to nap in the passenger seat of Giulia's car, but I couldn't. She was too busy singing along to Ariana Grande.

"Isn't that music, like, for teenagers?" I said, waking up from my sleep by another pop beat.

"That attitude of yours sure does remind me of a teenager," said Giulia.

"Ouch!" I replied.

"Besides," added Giulia. "She's Italian. It's patriotism."

"You know," I said, "I think Adrian is thinking about Italy."

We were pulling into the driveway.

"What does anyone know what Adrian's thinking?" said Giulia as she switched off the engine. "Besides," she added. "Big bro's off in New York, doing his business thing."

"Do you know why he had to leave?" I asked.

"Yeah. You'll never believe it. IRS. He's getting audited."

What! Why didn't he tell me?

"No way! Adrian's no cheat. He wouldn't be involved in anything like that."

"No. Trust me. He's so smart that he does his taxes like, five years in advance. Takes him about a day. I mean, if he did do anything wrong, there's no way they're gonna find it. Gotta watch that boy. *Fuoco.*"

"*Fuoco?*" I said.

"Something Mama used to say. About how he was fiery."

"He sure is." The depth of my tone surprised me.

Shit!

"Huh?" replied Giulia.

"Nothing," I said.

"Can I ask you about something?" said Giulia after a short while.

"Sure you can!" I replied, getting out of the car and stretching my legs. Giulia followed. She trotted up to the porch steps and sat beside me. "As long as it's not about what I've touched at the hospital."

Giulia smiled, but then her expression became a little serious. "Your mom called," she said.

I looked at her. *Oh no.*

"She said that you and Adrian were out. Like, together."

Mom, how could you, I thought. "Yeah... We were just talking. I mean, you know me, I like to be friendly, and we...I mean, I didn't know what you'd think, so I didn't really..."

Giulia was fixing me with a gaze. It was dreamy, like she was trying to imagine something.

Was she trying to imagine Adrian and me together?

"Whatever. Sorry. It's just your mom sounded worried about you. That's all."

"The only thing my mom needs to worry about is minding her own business," I said.

"Don't say that Zoe!" Giulia said a little loudly.

"Sorry, I didn't mean to..."

"Family is everything. I mean, Adrian's all the family I've got. And your mom's still alive and healthy and, God willing, will be for the next hundred years."

"I know. I'm so damn lucky. I know that. It's just, sometimes, she gets in the way."

"Well, nothing should ever get in the way of your family," said Giulia. "Not friends. Definitely not boyfriends."

I looked down. I felt like the secret was going to burst out of me. A dark cloud was coming over me, and I just had to tell her, but before I could open my mouth...

"Hey, guys. How are we doing today?"

I looked up into Wesley's face.

He was standing there, looking normal. If anything, he was back to his old self, still dressed in his dark t-shirt, ripped jeans, and boots. The ensemble wasn't exactly in line with my personal style, but I had to admit, it suited Wesley—the little dark cloud on the edge of our lives.

"Hi, Wes," said Giulia. "What are you doing?"

"Well, guess that depends on what you guys are doing," said Wesley, with a smile. "Sorry I haven't been around lately. Been kind of busy with work."

"Weren't you in Giulia's house on Tuesday?" I said.

Wes ignored the remark and carried on.

"How was the school week, Jules?"

"Giulia. Not Jules. And it was fine," said Giulia, a little tersely. She wanted Wes to go away. As a matter of fact, I wanted Wes to go away. Either that or I wanted him to explain how he managed to be everywhere he wasn't wanted at the moment.

"Guess I might see you later," Giulia said when Wes didn't respond.

Wes looked a little annoyed. "You guys don't wanna hang out?"

"Actually, we've hung out already today. Giulia and I have

been out and about." Try as I might, my damn smiley personality meant I couldn't stop making conversation. "We went to the gym, then the nail bar, then we got coffee," I said in a sing-song way.

Giulia moved her leg to the left, and it bumped into mine. At first, I thought it was by accident, but then I realized she was trying to stop me from blabbering on while she tried to ice Wes out.

"Well, I stopped by to let you know that I'm moving out tomorrow," said Wes. "Onto a new job in Arkansas."

"Really?" I said. Secretly, I was a little thankful that this was the last we'd see of him.

"Yeah," said Wes. "So, what are we doing to say goodbye?"

It was a combination of pitiful and awkward. "Wes," I said, "I'd like to help you celebrate and send you off, but I'm kind of tired. And I'm working tomorrow."

"It's Sunday tomorrow," spat Wesley.

"They need nurses on Sundays too, Wes. People need taking care of every day of the week."

"What Zoe's saying..." Giulia cut in, "...is that we're not doing anything with you today." I'd been trying to be nice and keep the peace, but Giulia had clearly snapped. She had no patience left with the guy who stood smugly grinning on her front lawn.

"That's not a very nice way to talk, *Jules*," said Wes.

"Don't call me that. And would you please just leave us alone?"

His expression darkened, and then I saw it again. That flicker of something in Wes' eyes that signaled he was becoming another person. Like, a completely different person. The socially awkward, shy nerd who I'd known vanished, and that confident, sly, dangerous creature was there.

"You smug fucking American girls," he muttered.

"What?" I said.

"I said..." he shouted, "...you smug fucking girls are gonna regret talking to me like that! You know that?! Do you have any idea who you're talking to!?"

I was frozen in fear at the rage Wes had suddenly unleashed, but Giulia had no such fear. She stood up in one moment and pointed to the left, where Wes' house was.

"Get the hell off my lawn," she said.

Wes snarled and made like he was about to take a step toward her. I shouted, "NO!"

Then, he relaxed.

"You might think twice before trusting your little friend there, Giulia. After all, she's been sleeping with your brother for the past month. Or maybe longer. Who knows with a girl like Zoe. *Puttana* (slut)."

He turned and walked slowly towards his house. He rounded the porch and went up the steps. We both looked away and heard the door slam.

My heart shattered. The heat outside suddenly became unbearable.

I looked at Giulia. She was breathing deeply. I could see that. But aside from that, I couldn't see any emotion on her face.

"*Is it true?*" she whispered.

I looked away. How could I tell her what I really felt—that I felt a way about Adrian that I'd never felt about anyone else?

"Yes," I said quietly.

Giulia stood up and went inside, closing the door behind her.

I sat on her step, hung my head, and let the tears fall.

Chapter 22

Adrian

On Saturday night, I got back to Cañon. It had been a tough three days. For the first two, I'd been dealing with the auditors. They wanted to look through everything. It was clear that whatever allegations had been made against me, they would have amounted to one of the greatest acts of financial fraud ever completed. By the time it was over, the meeting room where I'd set the guys up contained over three hundred thousand pages of data, spreadsheets, and files. The printing costs were in the thousands of dollars, and on Friday afternoon, when the guy begrudgingly admitted that I was squeaky clean, I handed him a bill for the printouts. As a matter of principle, Uncle Sam was going to foot the cost for this unfair invasion of my time and privacy.

The next eighteen hours were spent dealing with the shareholders and investors. I had over three hundred calls to make, personally assuring the people who'd poured money into my fund that I was, in fact, not a crook. While FINRA still had its own investigation to do, we could rest easy. And as I left the office at lunchtime on Saturday, there were more than a few apologies from my team, some of whom had doubted me more than I wanted to believe.

With that out of the way, there remained one question. Why? Why had someone tried to do this to me?

That would have to wait until I got home.

I texted Giulia, hoping that she'd give me some news about Zoe on the way. Instead of the usual set of three kisses, I got an uncharacteristic message from Giulia.

Can I come over?

*

Giulia settled herself in one of my armchairs by the fireplace. I didn't have it lit—it was a hot night—but she accepted a cup of coffee. I carried the cups down the long corridor between the living room and the kitchen, and we sat, by the light of the reading lamp, for a little while.

"Why do you live in a place like this?" said Giulia. "So drafty and old. You're like a vampire."

I laughed. "Is that what you came here to talk about?"

Giulia leaned over and put her coffee down.

"Today, Wesley came over. You know. That guy who lives next door."

"Today? I thought this was on Tuesday."

"Hear that from Zoe?"

"No...I..." I hesitated.

"So, who else did you hear it from?"

I looked down at my feet. I didn't know what to tell her. Or, more accurately, I didn't know why I never told her.

"I don't want to talk about that now," said Giulia. "I wanted to talk to you about something else."

"What?"

"Mom."

"Funny you say that. I was thinking about her myself the other day. I don't know why."

"I know why."

I peered at her.

"Something Mom did a long time ago. It's coming back, isn't it?"

"What do you mean?"

"Oh, come *on*, Adrian!" Giulia flapped her hands wildly, then settled down and sighed. "All these damn years, you never talk about her. You do everything you can. But you remember, don't you? You remember Italy?"

"I don't remember Dad, if that's what you're asking. He died when you were inside Mom. I was barely old enough to have any memories at all."

"Adrian," said Giulia. "You've always been so smart. How could you be so dumb about this? There's a reason for it all, isn't there?"

I looked at her. "A reason for what?"

"There's a reason Mom came from Italy! There's a reason she brought us! There's a reason she changed our name! What kind of Italian do you meet called 'Lawson'?"

"Obviously, she changed it because she wanted us to fit in."

"She didn't want to fit in, you dumbass! *SHE WANTED TO*

HIDE US!"

Giulia's voice echoed a little around the high, stone ceiling of my living room. Finally, it settled, and in the silence, I could hear the sounds of the night, cicadas singing, and the occasional call of a bird.

"You're crazy," I said. "How do you know?"

"I don't know, Adrian, I feel. Don't you remember what Mama was like when we asked her about the old country? When we asked to speak Italian with her? When she'd call you Adriano by mistake? When she'd insist I use Julia instead? She was terrified. She was terrified because something happened to our father, which meant she was somehow in danger. Isn't it obvious?"

I thought for a minute, and then I looked into her eyes.

"Complete this phrase," I said. "What is closed..."

"...Holds the secret!" said Giulia. "She used to say it all the time! Like when we moved into our old house, and there was that basement door that didn't move, that's what she said."

"When I was lying about something, and she knew I wasn't telling the truth..."

"When she was opening jars..."

"It had to mean something."

"Sure. But what?"

We thought for a minute in silence. I thought about it. So did Giulia, screwing up her face in the way she did when she was deep in concentration.

Silence ticked over the house, and eventually, I reached up to scratch my neck.

My nails gently knocked against the gold pendant.

I pulled it out of my neck.

"Mom gave this to me," I said. "She always said it belonged to Dad."

"Open it," said Giulia.

"It doesn't open."

Does it?

I looked at the pendant again, carefully. You'd expect to see a hairline crack down the side of the thing if it was possible to open it. I'd imagined that if it did open, it swung out like one of those old-timey watches or a locket.

But what if the seam—the join—was somewhere else?

I lifted it off my neck and turned it over.

"No way," said Giulia. "I tell you, that was one clever lady."

The back of the pendant did have a small, vertical line running down it. I looked at it. I dug a fingernail into the crack, but I couldn't get the leverage to pull it outwards.

"There's something there," I said, "but it doesn't work."

"Give it here," said Giulia.

As I handed it to her, the pendant glittered in the lamplight. I'd always been precious about handing it over to anyone.

Giulia tried to pry it open too.

"Be careful," I said. She was tugging at the only remaining thing I could connect with my father.

"I'm being careful," she said. "But it doesn't budge."

"Wait. Give it back."

I took it from her, in my hand. Sure, the pendant didn't open like a door. But that didn't mean there was no compartment inside.

I placed my thumb on the left slide and pinched the pendant on the other in my hand.

It slipped open.

"No way!" said Giulia.

Inside was a folded scrap of paper, yellowed and faded with the years. Protected from oxidation and dust inside the pendant, it had survived at least twenty years since the day Mom gave it to me.

I took it out and put the pendant on the table. It was so small I could hold it between my finger and thumb. I remembered that my mother worked as a jeweler in New York. She would know how to make something like this, or knew someone who could do it for her, at least.

I put it down, and unfolded it. I unfolded it again. It was half the size of a dollar bill now.

I unfolded it one last time and read the words written on there in a grave cursive, in soft, blue ink which had faded a little over time.

Adriano,

I don't know when this message will come to you or if it will come to you. The information is so terrible, so sad, that I entrust your finding it into the hands of fate. "What is closed, holds the secret." But it is up to us to open that which is closed.

You may remember your mother had a small, leather-bound book. I told you it was a photograph album when you were young. It is not an old photograph album. It was my journal. If you have finally discovered the secret inside this closed locket, then you are old enough to know where you have come from. The combination on the lock is 8, 4, 5, and 2. Turn the key left, then right, then left, then right, in each direction, and the journal will open for you.

I left this here for you so that if ever you and Giuliana were without me, you should know how to find out where you are from. I have tried to keep it from you for years, but there may come a day when your homecoming is a reality.

God Bless you and protect you, my most cherished children.

With all my love in the world,

Mama.

I put the letter down, and Giulia hopped over to the sofa with me, where she could read it. "Mama," she said, "Oh, Mama," and began to cry on my shoulder.

I wanted to pretend none of this had happened, and it had been put in the fire. But Mama was right. Fate had determined I was going to find out. Because my phone was ringing again. It was Reed.

"This is not a good time for me, again," I said drily.

"I figured, but I'm driving to your house right now."

"What?"

"Dr. Lawson, before we go any further, I'd just like to say I think you should get your family out of Cañon City and go. I'll be calling the cops right after I've spoken to you. Honestly, I'm amazed I haven't called them already."

"What? What do you mean?"

"I'll be at your place in ten minutes."

*

Duncan Reed, the P.I., sat in my room, fingering his lapels nervously.

"The man in the photograph? The one we couldn't ID? At first, I couldn't find him. He shouldn't be in the country. He's a ghost, as far as I'm concerned. No record of him arriving, no nothing."

"And Wesley Banks?"

"That's just it. Wesley Banks doesn't exist, either. But someone must be renting that house, I reckoned. So, I went to look. The house is rented under a different name. Paul De Luca."

"That's an Italian name," said Giulia. I looked at her. "Where's Zoe right now?"

Giulia stood and went into the hall, phone in hand.

"Whoever this guy is, he's an identity thief then. We know that now. I'll bet if you check his *record* of employment with the company..."

"There is no company. As far as I can tell, that office he rents on the other side of town? Dead. Wesley Banks—or, should I say, Paul De Luca—doesn't have a single client in Cañon City. He must have a pretty good tech setup, though. I tapped his wireless router. Guy's got a hell of a security network."

"I guess now we know who hacked my email account and my security system. And who's been responsible for manipulating

Vance's identification."

"There's another thing."

Reed's face looked grim. I recognized his expression. It was the one he had when we first met, when he assumed I was just another jealous husband. It was the face you get when you spend all day looking at family secrets.

"I finally have some information on Estella Lawson. At first, I didn't know where to look. But this morning, while I was searching for De Lucas…"

I already knew what he was going to say next.

"Well, she arrived here twenty-nine years ago with two small children. I know because Estella had to fill out a customs form."

"For declaring things? What was she carrying?"

"A hundred thousand dollars in cash, Dr. Lawson."

I flinched. *Where did my mother get that kind of money?*

"Estella also filed to change her name by deed poll. From De Luca, to Lawson."

"No."

"It seems too good to be true, doesn't it?"

I thought about Wesley, and how similar we looked. Was he a secret child of my mother's? Did I have a brother I didn't know about?

"Then," said the detective, "everything came together."

He took out the photograph he'd shown me before, of Vance speaking to the mysterious man in Rouse Park. Next to it, he placed a photo of a well-dressed man, in a suit, standing on a step. I recognized the man he was standing next to.

"That's the Italian prime minister."

"Right. And that..." said Reed, pointing at the man next to him, "...is Giovanni De Luca. He's an Italian businessman. Owns a series of hospitals. No convictions. His operation's worth hundreds of millions of Euros."

"And what," I said. "Are you telling me that this is my father?"

"No," said the P.I., looking away. "Your mother's maiden name was Cimbale. Your father, Stefano De Luca..." Reed said, "...we have a death certificate for. I'm getting a copy forwarded from the authorities. He died thirty years ago."

I watched his face. I wanted to tell him to get the fuck out of my house.

But somehow, I knew it was true. Every word.

"Adrian, this is your uncle. And, in legal terms, I have no way of proving he was ever on American soil."

I turned around and saw Giulia, frantically dialing her phone.

She turned to me, eyes wide.

"She's not picking up, Adrian. Zoe isn't picking up."

Chapter 23

Zoe

Ahead of me, in the distance, I could see him. Adrian was walking ahead of me. Taller and lankier since that first summer when we'd met.

I loved the way he walked. In summer, he walked with his short-sleeved shirt and a pair of smart, black pants. He was always smartly dressed, but not in a nerdy way. In a way that made him seem serious, academic. He looked like the film directors and actors in the books and magazines Giulia and I liked to read. I imagined how he might talk to me and turn around and notice me one day.

It was winter now, and the nights after school were dark and murky. I shivered against the cool air, and looked ahead, pulling my bag a little tighter over my shoulders.

Ahead of me, Adrian had disappeared around the block. I followed him, picking up my pace to a light jog. I didn't want to miss him, I needed to catch a glimpse of him.

I couldn't remember when I'd first started following home the boy who lived next door, the boy whose sister was rapidly becoming my best friend. It had happened over time, gradually.

Sometimes, being the happy, smiley person who tried to make everyone feel good was hard. For one, you were constantly surrounded by people. Whether it was because they liked you or because they wanted to talk to someone who would make them feel good, you were rarely alone in life. But where was the space to feel the things you felt which weren't happy and smiley? Where could you go to be alone, to lose yourself?

For me, that place was here. I watched Adrian walk home from school. We could have walked together if I'd asked him. I'm sure he would have thought it only polite to escort a lady home. Even though he was sixteen, he was old-fashioned that way.

In a few years, he'd graduate, and then I wouldn't be able to follow him at all. Giulia wondered why we never walked home from school together. This was why.

Ahead of me, round the corner, he was approaching the house. Every time Adrian got home, he jogged up the steps of the old-school porch, the kind with a covered roof and a balcony. He slipped his key into the lock and disappeared inside.

"What did he do in there all day?" I asked Giulia once.

"Mostly just looks at these old books mom has. They're like, medical textbooks."

"Was your mom a doctor?"

When I asked that, Giulia would look at her shoes.

"I don't know," she'd say curiously.

Once I saw Adrian go into his house, I'd always stop and slow down. Usually, Giulia would have caught up to me by then, and we'd walk the last two hundred yards or so to our houses together. But this time, she didn't. And I was left thinking about the handsome, dark boy, whose solitude provided me solitude, whose constantly sulky nature was a refuge for my own, over-happy heart.

I was almost home, but I hadn't seen the way there was a crack in the sidewalk. It happened a lot in summer but rarely in Winter. The local authority kept going on about how the entire road needed to be redone. I barely listened to my father's rants about it.

As I walked over the crack, I must have slipped. I fell, and as I did, I heard an awkward, crunching sound as pain filled my knee.

"ZOE!"

It was Adrian. Running to meet me. He was boyish as he sped across the front lawn of his house and straight across the front lawn of mine to meet me, where I lay sprawled on the pavement.

"Are you okay?" He helped me up, and I winced as I extended my leg.

"You're hurt," he said, and I could see a flash of concern in his eyes.

"Oh, no, really, I'm just fine!" I said, smiling through the pain.

"Your knee's all cut up. Come on. Let me help you with that."

I sat on the steps of his house, feeling about as stupid and embarrassed as it was possible to feel. Though Adrian was just two years older than me, I felt like a little girl as he took out the medical kit his mother kept under the sink and brought it to me. He wiped the knee and put a plaster on.

"There you go."

*

A noise woke me. I sat up, where I'd fallen asleep on the sofa.

Had I been dreaming, or had I been remembering? I could hardly tell. I remembered the day in detail—Adrian running to meet me, nervously bandaging my wound. I also remembered one of his trademark grumpy tantrums afterward about how I had to be careful. And yet, I'd been asleep.

I looked at my phone. It was late. I'd put it on silent—I didn't want anyone disturbing me. I went to check the screen for notifications when I heard another noise. What had woken me up in the first place? It sounded like a car engine. But this noise sounded more muffled. Like a voice whispering.

I looked around me. There was no one in the house.

My heart began to beat a little faster. I got up from the sofa slowly. The window on the side of the house, the one with a view of Wes' front lawn, might hold a clue as to who was outside. I was nervous now after Wesley's threat.

Do you have any idea who you're talking to? He had said.

Slowly, I looked out through the side window.

I screamed.

When I say I screamed, I mean, I really screamed. I hollered at the top of my voice. I stepped back, shocked by the volume issuing out of my mouth on pure instinct. A shot of adrenaline coursed through my body, and suddenly, I was in fight-or-flight mode. Someone was looking in through my window, a dark figure dressed in black.

I stepped back again into the hallway and crouched.

That was when the door came off the handles.

The thundering crack split the doorframe, and I watched in sheer horror as the door came down. The man in the doorway was big, and he wore a ski mask. I yelped and stepped backward as the top of my door landed where I'd been standing a moment ago.

The figure in the doorway crouched, as if to pounce.

"GET THE HELL AWAY FROM ME, YOU PSYCHO!" I cried as it stepped in.

It said something to me, but behind the mask, all I heard was a dangerous roar.

I kicked and flailed backward as it came before I fell down. I was on the stairs now. Jumping up, I turned and fled, but the figure leaped up and grabbed my ankle as I did.

I screamed again and fell down, juddering down a few of the steps. The man attacking me was trying to drag me down.

I turned and, out of luck rather than skill, managed to land a kick right in his face. I winced and cried out in pain as my foot collided with the plastic of the ski mask, but at least it had knocked him backward.

Behind him, the other figure—the one I'd seen at the window—appeared in the doorway. There were two of them.

I jumped up, and this time, I sprinted up the stairs. But I didn't have long. They were coming after me.

I turned around, clawing the banister, trying not to slip on the polished floor, and within seconds, I was barreling through the doorway to my bedroom. My momentum was so great I could hardly stop. I rolled over the bed and fell down on the other side.

I heard their thundering footsteps, and then they were in the open doorway. I had nowhere to go. I stood, turning briefly to look out of the window, hoping for a passerby.

But the moonlit street below was empty.

No one was coming to help.

"Enough of this shit," said one of them and pulled a gun from his pocket. "Don't move. Or I'll shoot you."

"Please...please..." I whimpered, pressing my back to the window. "Don't hurt me."

"We're not gonna hurt you, sweetheart," said the man, pulling off his ski mask.

It was the detective.

"Vance?" I said in disbelief. "You..."

"We just wanna borrow you," he said. "Dr. Lawson's got something we need."

Chapter 24

Adrian

I kept the journal in a box with the rest of my mother's things. I'd gone upstairs to fetch it, but by the time I came back down, Giulia had her shoes and her jacket on. Duncan Reed, the PI, had already left to go make a statement at the neighboring county's police department.

"I've got all the evidence here..." he said, "...but still, they won't believe me."

"I'm very grateful for what you're doing."

"Grateful enough to let me write a book about it?" grinned Reed before he left.

That was 10 minutes ago.

"What are you doing?" I asked Giulia.

"I'm going down the hill," she said.

"What?" I said. Then, I thought of my mother. What would she say if I let my sister go out, all on her own?

"Wait!" I cried, as Giulia made for the door.

"There's no time," she replied. "Zoe's in trouble."

"I can't let you go out alone," I said. "You could be hurt or injured. Vance and Wesley—or Paul, or whatever his name is—could be after us! You could get killed."

"Mom wouldn't want us to leave Zoe behind," said Giulia, shaking her head and turning around.

"Mom would tell me to put you first, above Zoe. Family first, remember?" I walked towards her, but what Giulia said next made my heart stop.

"Zoe IS family!" said Giulia. "I love her. She's my best friend. And she was with me at the funeral."

I sighed. If Giulia only knew the truth of what we'd done that day.

"Giulia, I...That day at the funeral. I was upset, and I didn't know what to do. Zoe came upstairs to fetch me and..."

"And what?" Giulia said fiercely. "You slept together?"

I nodded. I felt so guilty.

"You think it's such an awful thing that you and Zoe are together," said Giulia, sighing. "But I think it's wonderful."

"You do?" I said, looking up. How could Giulia think like that?

"You shouldn't have lied to me," she said. "And you shouldn't have kept lying, letting the lies build and build like now. If not, Zoe would be here with us now. She'd be safe. And because of your lies, she's down there, in her house, next to that goddamn psychopath."

Giulia was right. Everything could have been prevented if we'd come clean sooner.

A combination of rage and shame and the revelation the PI had made were combining to give me a furious headache. My mood was dark, but she was right.

I needed Zoe. Without her, I didn't know what I'd be. I hardly knew who I was anymore. How had I become so wrapped up in myself and my problems that I'd let the woman who meant as much to me as my sister get into danger?

I love her.

There were no questions about that.

"I'll be quick," said Giulia. "I'll go with Chris; he'll drive me there and back. I'll bring her here, nice and quickly. Shouldn't be any trouble."

Once she'd left, I locked the door behind her. There was no point taking any chances. Someone might come for me. And that someone might be coming to take the leatherbound journal by any means necessary.

I opened it, using the combination from the note inside my pendant. I turned to the first page. It was dated from thirty-three years ago. My Italian was hardly up to the standard of the book, but I struggled through it. It seemed to have been written shortly after my mother's honeymoon.

Today I thank God, because I just found out I am pregnant. Stefano is delighted. If it's a boy, we will name him Adriano, after his grandfather. If it's a girl, we will call her Giuliana, after my mother. That way, Stefano and I have a 50/50 chance of getting to pick the baby's name.

Stefano has returned to work at the hospital, but he is concerned. He and Giovanni are fighting again. Brothers shouldn't fight, but Giovanni is so young and hot-headed. Will he learn his place in the family?

I couldn't make out the passage below; the language was too difficult. But it seemed to indicate that there was something about the business in the hospital that Giovanni didn't understand. He was too naïve or hot-headed to see what it was.

I skimmed a few pages.

I thought when I came to Tuscany that my life would be boring. It's turning out to be quite the opposite!

I haven't had a chance to write in this diary for such a long time. The work of a mother is never done (as my own likes to remind me every time I call her on the phone)! Adrian is healthy and well. I know he's going to grow up to be a strong boy. His second birthday was today, and, I have news. I am pregnant again! The doctors tell me she's a little girl. So, according to Stefano's terms, Giuliana will arrive in the world not too soon.

Yesterday after church, we went to a party at Stefano's father's home. The old man is as spry as ever, so it was funny that at this dinner, he asked Stefano to give a speech on his behalf. It turns out Stefano will inherit the company once his father passes away! Isn't that nice? Everyone was there, except, of course, Giovanni.

I flipped forward to the next entry, and as I did, I felt sick to my stomach. I knew what was coming, of course, but the woman who'd written in this diary had no idea.

Today the road leading from the house is closed, and policemen are walking up and down the driveway.

My darling, darling Stefano is gone. He died last night. They say it was a car accident.

The sparseness and the way the words were written on the page led me to think my mother had never finished the entry. I thought that was it—the rest of the journal, fifty or so pages—looked blank. So that was it. My mother had stopped writing when my father passed away. But then I turned back and looked at the entry.

They say it was a car accident.

I flicked forward a few pages, and then, when I thought there was nothing left to read, I saw my mother's writing again. Only this time, her swooping cursive hand seemed cramped, as if written in a hurry.

It was Giovanni. I knew it. He came to me this afternoon while I was watching Adriano play in the garden and sat on the bench where I was knitting.

"Do you know, Estella," he said, "the terms of my bastard father's will? It has a fidecomissium. Do you know what that is?"

I kept silent and said nothing. I couldn't stand the sight of him.

"My little Paul," he said, "is going to get nothing of those damned hospitals. None of the money will be his after I die. I can store as much of the profit away as I want, but as soon as little Adriano turns eighteen...it will return to

him."

I looked at my son playing in the garden. Giuliana was inside the house with the nurse.

"He's a little boy," I said. "He doesn't know anything. How could you threaten to hurt him?"

"I'm threatening no one," said Giovanni, but his eyes said otherwise.

On the final page of the journal, at the very end, where no one would see from a casual glance, the following was written.

Giovanni has made his intentions clear. Last night the gardener saw a man approaching through the back lawn. He waved him off, but I know they will come again. Little Adriano—and his sister—are not safe while that man is still alive. He will hunt them to the ends of the earth if he can. I must leave for America and take the children with me. I will set a fire to the house—we'll be presumed lost or missing presumed dead. Giovanni will take the estate—he can have it, for all I care, as long as my babies are safe. I withdrew the last of Stefano's money—that will tide us over until I can find a job. I was once a humble jeweler's assistant before I became the wife of a wealthy man. I'll become that woman again for the sake of my son. I'm locking this journal with a combination only I know. That way, Adriano will never discover who he really is. Not until the time's right.

The book fell from my hands. Devastated, I dropped to the marble floor.

"Why, Mama?" I said. "Why did he do this to you?"

My mother had brought us to America and raised us never to know the terrible reason she had left. Giovanni—my uncle—had killed my father for control of the estate. Now, he was coming after me to make sure I never returned.

On the back page of a journal was a sealed envelope stamped with a royal flourish. I opened it. It was some kind of legal document, though one I wasn't able to read.

I bet it was a copy of the will, before it had been altered to favor Giovanni's firstborn son after my presumed death. I was holding a will that signified me as the rightful heir of my father's estate. I wasn't Adrian Lawson. I was Adriano De Luca, from one of the most successful medical families in the world.

My phone was ringing. I picked it up, expecting to hear Giulia's voice.

"*Ciao*, Adriano. It's me. Do you recognize my voice?"

He had been clever. He'd played the fool, the clown, a shy, socially awkward man. He'd disguised his accent and buried everything—his whole personality—in order to fool us. I knew now that the man on the phone was the one who'd taken the keys and vandalized my car. It was him who'd hacked my emails, my security system, and who'd falsified Vance's documentation.

"*Ciao*, Wesley," I said. "Or, is that Paul?"

"Very good. We knew you'd figure it out eventually." His accent was thick. There was no point pretending anymore.

"I must say, I'm surprised you're calling me, Paul," I said. "I'm surprised you did any of this. After all, if you'd let me and my sister be, I wouldn't be in the process of figuring out how best to explain all this to the police."

"Oh, Adriano," said my cousin. "I wish it were that simple. I really do. But you see, someday you would have found out. And even if not now, in thirty or fifty years. And then it would be your children, or your children's children, who took back what was rightfully theirs. All we wanted at first was for you to be frightened, move on, change your name, whatever. But now..." he said, "...now that you know, we don't have a choice. You really think you can have my father followed, and we won't know? This way, Papa says, we cut the plant at its root."

"You're not cutting anything," I said. "My private investigator's on his way to report you to the police right now. And I'll be doing the same."

"I'm trembling," said Paul sardonically. "Of course, there is one problem."

"What's that?"

"Zoe won't see the sunrise if that happens."

I froze. *They've got her.*

"You lying bastards," I said.

"Am I lying?" said Paul. "Here, bitch. Cry for your puppy dog!"

I heard a scream, and wailing, like a gag had been removed. "Let go of me, asshole!" I recognized the voice immediately. It was Zoe.

"You can't do this," I protested.

"I can, and, for the sake of my family," said Paul, "I will. Now, to business. You want to see her alive again, don't you?"

"Yes," I said. It was taking everything I had not to throw the phone down on the floor, but now I had one priority: keeping Zoe safe.

"You have something my father wants, Adriano. It's a will. The last copy, in fact."

"And say I find this will," I said, resisting the urge to scream. "What happens then?"

"I'll call you, and we'll make the trade, of course."

"All right, you bastard, but I'm warning you. Don't try anything."

Giulia burst through the door of my house ahead of me. She was in tears. "ADRIAN!" she cried. "Her house...it was all torn up. They've taken her! They've taken Zoe!"

"Sounds like word's spread fast," chuckled Paul. "You'd better hope your, uh, what's the word—gumshoe—hasn't reached the police yet."

I hung up.

"We'll get her back," I said to Giulia. I was comforting myself just as much as her.

Chapter 25

Zoe

I don't know whether I fainted or whether they knocked me unconscious. For the longest time, I was aware of nothing, except a faint feeling of bumping around, like I might have been in the back of a car.

After a while, I felt the wind on my face and the heat of the night. But then, I suddenly started to come to.

I was in a cold, draughty space. From the looks of it, I guessed I was in a warehouse somewhere on the outskirts of the city. I thought I saw a row of windows tinged with an eerie blue light up above me. But I couldn't see anything because of the enormous, bright floodlights that shone on me. With a mixture of horror and fascination, I recalled the moment when, in the driveway, I'd seen Wesley hauling me into the back of his car.

They'd been planning this for days.

All that equipment.

He'd been visibly taunting me with it all.

I was kneeling on the dirty, bare floor of the place. Ahead of me, behind the lights, I saw a shadow move across the light.

It was the Detective. Vance, or whatever his name was.

I tried to call out to him, to tell him to help me and untie me, before I remembered that I was gagged. I couldn't say anything. The thick tape they'd put over my mouth made it hard to breathe, and I started to panic for a moment. But then I took big breaths and started to heave sobs.

"Nothing personal, sweetheart," said the detective. He was sitting on an upturned milk crate. I watched him put a cup of coffee down on the ground beneath him and pull off his gloves. "Wasn't our intention to hurt you. It's your little boyfriend we're after."

His attitude was frighteningly casual. I realized that Vance was nothing like the person I assumed he'd be.

"I should know better than anyone," he said, "how scary things can get. You know they sent me to prison?"

I looked at him. Maybe by listening to him, I could understand him. Or at least let him talk and get free.

"Life in prison ain't exactly too good for a cop. It's a miracle I survived, really. I spent eighteen years locked up. And the worst part? It ain't even Adrian Lawson's fault."

My eyes were scanning the building, looking for exits. I would occasionally shut them to avoid the glow of the floodlights while he spoke. But occasionally, I turned to look at Vance, wondering if I could stand up and run past him.

"I'd just made detective," Vance began, "and we were working a burglary. A jewelers on 59th Street. We arrived on the scene and saw a few valuables had been stolen. So, hell, I thought to myself: 'they're insured. They're going to get the money back. Why don't I just help myself?' So let's say a few priceless diamonds the thieves themselves were too dumb to steal went missing from the store. What can I say? I had a wife and a kid to feed. They don't exactly pay a detective all that much, you know. It's not like we were going on fancy vacations every year. God, the rich do keep getting richer, don't they?

"Only problem is, Adrian Lawson's mom was showing us around at the time. And she saw me swipe 'em. I don't know how she did—I was clever—but she mentioned it to my colleague.

"Unfortunately, the judge didn't look too kindly on me tampering with the crime scene. So what if the goddamn thieves were never caught," said Vance, railing and throwing his arm around. "So what?"

I could see that he'd been drinking. I'd wager there was more than just coffee in the mug he rose to his lips and took a sip from.

"Eighteen years," Vance said, shaking his head. "For a few necklaces and diamond rings. So you see, sweetheart," he said, turning and looking at me sullenly, "for me, what you and your doctor boyfriend are going through isn't so bad at all. It ain't gonna cost you your job. It ain't gonna cost you your livelihood. See it from my perspective?"

I didn't see it at all, but I was more clever than that. I nodded.

"That's a good girl," said Vance. "Want me to take that gag off?"

"You sure as hell aren't gonna do that," said a voice behind me.

It was Wesley. Or, it was the person—the creature—I'd thought Wesley was. He circled me now, and I could see he had been behind me for some time, hidden by the floodlights. Even if I could have stood up with my hands tied behind my back, even if I could have run away from Vance, there was no way I'd manage to get away from Wes. His voice had changed now—not only did he speak more confidently, more clearly, but he also had a heavy

Italian accent.

"I need her nice and quiet for a bit," he said, "while I make a phone call."

It took me a while to realize he was calling Adrian, telling him how he could get me back. I shook my head. Adrian would never come. Not while he had to protect Giulia. At one point, Wes stalked over and slapped me hard. "Here, bitch," he said. "Cry for your puppy dog!"

I cried out as he ripped the tape off, then he stalked away and finished his conversation. After he did, he came back.

"Is he on his way?" said Vance, sulkily. "I kinda want to get my fee and go. You hear me, Paul? They're expecting me in the sheriff's office tomorrow."

Paul?

Even his name was a lie.

"You'll get yours when the job is done," Paul said. I could see in the light of the floodlights that he was utterly unhinged, crazy. He looked unslept now, at his wit's end.

"What do you want?" I said weakly. They hadn't put back the gag. It took a few swallows to perch my dry throat.

"What do I want?" said Paul, imitating me in a whiny, high-pitched voice. "I want the will. The will which identifies Adrian as the heir of the De Luca fortune."

"The what?" I said. I couldn't understand this—any of it.

"Poor Zoe," he replied. "Head empty as a bowl. Don't worry. You'll get to see Adrian again. Before I shoot him dead, once he's given me what I want, that is."

"NO!" I cried. "You're a monster, you freak, you sicko!"

"Now, now," he said, "you American girls don't got no respect for a man."

"I don't have any respect for you. And if you think Adrian's just gonna roll over and let you take his money, his family name, then you've got another thing coming," I spat.

"We'll see, Zoe," said Paul. "We'll see."

*

After what seemed like a hundred years, Vance shook himself into action. "I'd better get into position," he said.

Paul took his place on the milk crate. He held a heavy, dark object in his right hand, which I realized was a gun. It sent chills through my body. I was numb, exhausted, and dehydrated, but all I could think of was Adrian. I'd rather die myself than let anything happen to him.

Even if I'd never get to hold him again.

Even if he didn't feel the same way about me as I did about him.

I loved Adrian.

I felt it then, and I whispered it to myself.

"What did you say?" said Paul.

"Nothing," I muttered.

"When my father told me I had a cousin," said Paul, "I was happy. 'Papa,' I said, 'there's a boy my age who I can play with, who I can tell stories to.' But I didn't know then."

"Why do you think I care about any of this?" I said.

"SHUT UP!" he screamed and raised the gun. Then, like a

puppet without its strings, he dropped back to the same posture he'd had before.

"You see," he said, "there is a law in my family's will. It says that only the firstborn son can inherit the fortune. My papa, he did this out of love for me. For me and for my children. That is why I came to America to help him. That is why I learned everything I could about computers so that I could make his plans a reality. That is why I will kill Adrian. For family. It's a concept few of you selfish Americans can understand."

"That's not true," I said. "Because Adrian's my family. He may be difficult, and we may fight, but I've known him for over sixteen years. And he's mine. Giulia too. We grew up next door to each other. We took care of each other. We never lied to each other. We never killed for each other."

"But you did lie to one another," said Paul, smirking. "I mean, to keep from his sister that the two of you shared a bed," he sneered, spitting. "Disgusting. I don't know what he sees in you."

"You know, Paul," I said. "When I first met you, I thought you were a shy, awkward guy who needed to be treated with kindness. I thought you were someone I could make friends with. Even when you started acting like a creep, I still thought there might be goodness in you."

He looked at me, emotionlessly.

"Now," I said, "I realize that you aren't shy, and you aren't awkward. But you're definitely a creep. You're a nauseating, self-centered creep who's killing, kidnapping, and extorting people because daddy told you to. You make me sick."

"I ought to KILL YOU!" he screamed, standing up.

"Simmer down, Paul," said Vance from somewhere above me. I couldn't see him in the shadows.

"Let's relax, Paul. After all, it's not her you're angry at, is it?"

I turned, craning my neck as far as it would go I nearly fell over. Adrian was almost buried in the gloom at the far end of the warehouse.

"Let her go, Paul," he said.

"Shoot!" Paul screamed. "He's here!"

"You asshole," said Adrian coolly. I looked at him. The gorgeous, strong man who'd changed my life stood ahead of me, facing imminent death, and all I could do was watch.

"Where is it? Your hands are empty! Don't play with me, *Adriano*!"

"As if I'd bring it in here," said Adrian. "That you up there, *Detective Vance*?"

I heard a growl from somewhere up above me on a metal gangway, and a shot was fired. It bounced off the ground.

"STOP!" screamed Paul. He was utterly demented. "YOU IDIOT! He doesn't have the will with him. Where is it, Adriano? Tell me now, or so help me, I'll blow you away."

"I figured you'd say that," said Adrian. "So I left the will with my sister."

"Fuck," hissed Vance. "He's double-crossed us."

"Excellent way of putting it, Vance."

I saw Paul reach up, aiming his gun at Adrian. I couldn't wait. Pitching forward onto my knees, I sprung up, and ran for him, my hands behind my back.

I knocked Paul over and saw him pitch forward. The gun clattered a few meters away from him. Another shot came, whizzing by my head.

"You bitch," said Paul, getting up as I struggled in the dirt. But then I saw Adrian dive forward.

If I'd managed to trip Paul up, Adrian knocked him off his feet. The pair sprawled together on the dusty ground. But Adrian was smart.

"I can't get a shot!" screamed Vance. "Paul! Move your ass!"

Adrian was strong, but Paul was too lithe, too crazy to be beaten. He rolled over and kicked Adrian in the eye. Adrian stumbled back. But next to him was Paul's pistol.

He grabbed it, cocked it and aimed it at Paul. "STOP!" yelled Adrian.

When he shouted, I felt it in my shoes. The whole warehouse heard it. Paul froze, his eyes darting around the room.

"Shoot the girl!" he yelled.

I spun and saw Vance taking aim.

"No!" cried Adrian.

I closed my eyes and braced myself for death.

"Drop it," said a voice I'd never heard before.

I looked up again. Next to Vance, on the gangway, was a man dressed in fairly unremarkable clothes. He was pointing a gun an inch from Vance's temple.

"Who in the hell are *you*?" said Vance.

"I'm Duncan Reed," the man answered. "Drop the gun. Now."

Chapter 26

Adrian

It was dawn by the time I finally realized that it was over.

After the cops had flooded the warehouse, I watched in a blur as Paul was taken away. As I saw them cart him out of there, handcuffed, I realized I was watching my cousin being led away.

I'd always been a little disturbed by Wesley's resemblance to me. But it was still shocking to realize that for months the stranger who had so cleverly worked his way into Giulia and Zoe's lives had been hiding in the United States under a secret identity. Wesley Banks was a fiction, an invention to disguise Paul's identity, and it had worked perfectly for the most part. We'd been so stunned by his resemblance to me that we hadn't even considered the possibility that he might really be a relation of ours.

I was worried for Zoe, but for the longest time, they wouldn't let me talk to her. The warehouse was a mess of DNA evidence.

That night, they interrogated me. I wanted to keep my secrets, but bit by bit, they spilled. I'd given Giulia the diary and the will for safekeeping should I not return from the warehouse. And she'd dutifully handed them over while I spoke to the detectives in charge of the case. In a darkened room, under a lamp that swung steadily from side to side like the pendulum of a clock, I confessed everything.

I confessed that my mother had brought us to the United States when we were small. That our real name wasn't Lawson—it was De Luca. And that whomever Giovanni was—the mysterious figure behind Paul's deception, the break-ins and intrusions I'd suffered over the last few months—he'd threatened my mother, and she'd left the country. My own family had conspired to betray me because of the terms of the will, the *fidecomissium*, which stated that I was the rightful heir to the fortune.

"What does Miss Hollis mean in all of this?" said one of the detectives, suspiciously.

"Zoe got caught up in what they were trying to do," I explained. "They were using her to get to me. They kidnapped her because they knew I'd go after her."

"And why *did* you go after her, Dr. Lawson?"

I hung my head. "Because I love her."

It was the truth.

After more questions, they explained to me who Detective Vance was—or wasn't. That documents had been found in his home, which identified him as a completely different person. Working under an assumed identity and assisted by Wesley—or Paul, or whatever you want to call him—Vance had transferred to the police department. His grudge against my mother for telling on him to the police had made him bitter and twisted by the years. All it took was for my uncle to prey on that bitterness and persuade him to help unravel my life.

By then, my lawyer had arrived. But it would take a long time before we could find the evidence to show that I'd been the victim of a terrible crime—not just in this country, but in the one I'd been born in. And it would take even longer until people in town stopped looking at me like I was the impostor.

Adrian Lawson wasn't any more real than Detective Vance, any more real than Wesley Banks. Just like them, he was the product of a secret, a terrible secret that had taken me from my home halfway across the world. I didn't really know myself at all.

I wasn't Adrian Lawson. I was Adriano De Luca.

They questioned me all night, taking my statements and listening to me tell my story. A story that sounded so impossible that I was hardly sure I believed it. When it got light outside, and I realized how exhausted I was, they asked me to stay at the police station in a cell. I wasn't safe being let back onto the streets. After all, my uncle could still have people looking for me.

"I don't care," I snarled wearily as the morning light began to poke through the dingy window of the station while they explained the situation to me. "I just want to know where Zoe is."

"She's fine, Adrian," said the detective. "And we're keeping her safe, believe me."

I kept asking to see her, but they wouldn't let me. Why? Did they think I was somehow a danger to Zoe? Because of what Paul had done? What my family had done to her?

Or was it that she didn't want to see me?

I'd found out who I was. But had I lost the woman I loved?

Two days later, they released me. I walked out into the hot sun, with the world looking strange and new.

I expected Giulia to be waiting for me outside the station, but she wasn't there. Nor was Zoe. Instead, my lawyer was waiting for me, along with Charlie. He stood by a hire-car along with the lawyer.

"Adrian," he said and jogged gently towards me. He gave me a hug. I was amazed. Did I look that bad? Then, I saw my reflection in the car window and gasped.

There were dark circles around my eyes, and they were a little sunken. I looked exhausted, and if it were possible, I'd say I'd lost a few pounds in the last couple of days. I looked haggard. But there was more to it than that. As much as I felt like me, there was a haunted look in my eyes.

I thought it would cheer me up, being with Charlie, who'd known me for years. But when we finished hugging, he looked at me with a dark expression.

"We need to talk," he said. And I knew it wasn't good news.

*

"What do you mean they're back?"

I stood in my living room. I hadn't had a chance to eat anything, and for once, I hadn't reached for a glass of whiskey to settle my nerves. Instead, I was sipping a glass of water while Charlie sat nervously on the sofa. My lawyer had taken out his briefcase, and the documents were scattered across the table.

"The IRS have come. Since the news broke, it's come to light that you're not exactly..."

He hesitated, and I finished for him.

"I'm not who I say I am?"

He nodded. "Your family's lived under the name Lawson for many years," he said. "But it isn't your real name. Your mom wanted to protect you, and name changes are legally binding documents that can be traced. If anyone wanted to find out who you really were..."

"Then they could just find the change by deep poll."

"Right. As you might understand, this has caused a bit of a misunderstanding. IRS has seized your office and frozen our accounts. Investors are trying to pull their money, claiming they've been the victim of a scam."

"There's no scam," I said. "Surely we can prove in court that I didn't know that my name is really De Luca."

"I hope so," chimed in Bryant Dallas, my lawyer. "But that could take a long time. In any case, should the court find in favor of your investors in the meantime..."

"We'll lose everything," I said, defeated. "What's the worst-case scenario?"

Charlie looked at the lawyer.

"At worst, Adrian," he said, "you're facing extradition. But we're going to fight this. Don't you worry. Everyone is behind you after what you've been through. But the word's out now, and we can't fight this. You need to embrace this...change."

I nodded. "Well, there is some good news," I said.

"What's that?"

"I've never liked my last name much."

Thus began the long, arduous process of clearing my name. Charlie and I worked out a strategy that day while I lay feeling exhausted and depressed on the sofa in the living room. We'd release the information to the press. The whole truth, and nothing but. I was my mother's son, but since she'd never told us that our name was De Luca, we could prove to the court that I was who I said I was. The diary would come in handy for that.

But currently, it was being used as evidence in a completely different case—the case of Zoe's kidnapping. And until Paul or Vance confessed, there was no way we'd be able to begin to fight our case.

It was going to take years to clear my name. Fortunately, I had options: money in escrow, offshore accounts, which was rightfully mine, and I could claim to keep me afloat.

But this whole affair was going to be the ruin of me.

After Charlie and my lawyer had given up and gone, I received two emails. My medical license had been suspended pending a fraud investigation due to the confusion on my identity. The second one was from the HR office at the hospital where I was suspended due to my license being suspended.

Talk about a domino effect.

There was nothing I could do and resigned myself to the situation for the moment.

That night, I slept a dreamless, dark sleep. I woke early and looked out of my bedroom window. The last time I'd slept here this easily, Zoe had been by my side.

Zoe. She was all I could think about. And yet I still hadn't called her. I was afraid of what she'd tell me—that I'd lied to her, pretended to be someone I wasn't. I didn't know what I'd do to make things right.

But I did know one thing. My days of hiding, of avoiding her, were over. I'd confronted the secrets of my past.

But if I didn't see Zoe, my future would go nowhere.

*

Later that next day, I drove into town. As I passed the rows of houses, my memory stretched back to a time when innocence and peace had been the norm along these roads. When I'd been at school, and come home to my mother's loving embrace. To Giulia. And to Zoe, the girl next door who'd fascinated me all my adult life.

The girl whose front door I was going to now.

When I got there, I was shocked. The front door, caved in, was barred by police tape. Outside they were still picking up pieces of broken glass, and splinters of wood. A cop car stood on the side of the street, and my heart ached, knowing what she'd gone through.

I hadn't been there to protect her.

All my life, I'd wanted to keep her safe. And any man who crossed her path had had to deal with me.

But this time, it was my fault that Zoe had been in danger. If I'd only spoken to her sooner, let her know what was coming, she might have been prepared for it.

How could I protect her from myself?

I parked on the sidewalk outside Giulia's house, and was surprised when I saw a cop car in the driveway. The two police officers were standing outside on the porch, discussing something, when I approached.

"Sir, I'm going to have to ask you to leave," said one of them, stepping down from the porch as they saw me approach.

"My sister's here," I said. "Surely you can let me in."

One of the cops frowned at me. "You're the doctor?" he asked. "The Italian?"

"The American," I growled. "And I'm here to see Giulia

Lawson."

The cop shrugged and nodded. He walked back from me up to the porch, where a walkie-talkie sat on top of a set of papers in a plastic wallet. He took the walkie-talkie and radioed someone else, speaking in a hushed tone for a few seconds.

"Miss Lawson and Miss Hollis are under police escort for the time being," he said. "Sorry. You can go in."

"Thanks," I replied, sarcastically.

The cop went inside for a moment, and when he came to the front door, it was with Giulia. When she saw me, she stopped dead in her tracks. And froze.

My sister had always worn her heart on her sleeve. It was one of her qualities I admired the most. But when she saw me, for the first time in my life, I didn't know whether she would hit or hug me.

It turned out, it was both.

Giulia ran towards me, and flung her arms around me. Then, she pulled back and began to punch my chest with her hands.

"You...stupid...idiot!" she said. "You could have...gotten yourself...killed!"

"Ma'am, please don't do that," said one of the cops from the porch, obviously concerned that Giulia was going to knock me out.

"*Vaffanculo!*" she cursed in response and turned and pounded on my chest with her fists.

"Easy, easy!" I said, and she finally stopped. There were tears in her eyes, and she flung her arms around me again, and sobbed.

"I hate you," she sniffled, and I laughed as I held her. "I love you. Mama would be so cross with you right now. And so happy."

She pulled back.

"You saved Zoe," she said.

"No, I didn't," I said.

"You *did*," she replied. "You saved *cara Zoe* from those bastards."

"I did what I had to do," I said. "Not that I'll ever see her again."

Giulia looked at me, like I'd come from another planet. "What do you mean?" she said. "She's in my garden now. You gotta come talk to her."

"What?"

"She's been staying over since they let her go from questioning. They're still gathering evidence from her house. You know, from when..."

Giulia looked like she was going to cry again, so I patted her arm. "Can I talk to her?"

"I don't know. Maybe. She's kind of quiet at the minute."

"Is she okay?"

Giulia snorted. "How would you feel? If some *bastardi* kidnapped you and held you hostage?"

"Okay," I said. "Please...I need to see her."

Giulia thought about it for a while. I'd lied to her as well, I kept telling myself. I hadn't told Giulia that Zoe and I had been meeting in secret, that when everyone had doubted me, she'd believed me, and it had made me cling tighter to her. Before we were separated. Before my temper got in the way and destroyed what we had together.

"Okay," she said. "Go into the garden."

The garden was warm, and the smells of Giulia's plants and the gentle whirr of insects made the atmosphere almost stifling. At the back door, I looked out and saw her, under a parasol, in a chair. She held a book in her hands and was still.

I stepped down from the back door, and a pair of soft, blue eyes lifted from the pages of the book and met mine. They widened, and then a silence fell over the garden.

For a while, I said nothing and stood drinking in the sight of Zoe. Her blonde hair had been tied up into a ponytail, and she sat in a light summer dress, a soft shade of blue. Were it not for the bruises on her arms, the cut above her eye where she'd fallen in the warehouse, which had needed a few stitches, she'd have looked just as beautiful as the day I walked back into her life that summer.

I stepped forward into the light, admiring her soft, bare legs and clever fingers as she folded her page and put the book down on the table. I saw her hands tremble, and she stood, defensive, wary of me.

"Adrian," said Zoe. It wasn't a question, just a statement, as if she was convincing herself that it was really me.

"Zoe," I replied.

Again, nothing. It was like two strangers had met. And indeed, in some ways, we were strangers, stepping out together into a world where neither of us would be the same again after what we'd gone through.

And yet, I recognized her lush, soft, blonde hair. I recognized her ample breasts and the curve of her back, which I'd kissed before and wanted nothing more than to kiss again. I could pick her out in a crowd of a thousand, easily. A crowd of a million.

She was one of a kind.

"I didn't know if you'd want to see me," I said.

Zoe's lower lip trembled, and she looked away. We both knew that I'd done her a terrible wrong. My actions might have saved her, but they also put her in danger.

"I'm sorry," I said, but the words meant nothing unless I explained it. So I did.

"I'm sorry I pushed you away," I began. "I'm sorry I didn't listen to you. I'm sorry I lied to you, and I'm sorry I lied to Giulia. I'm sorry I never told you what I was doing or where I was going. And I'm sorry I never listened to you because you, Zoe...you mean the world to me. You mean so much. I never meant to let you down, but I've carried this weight with me for years..."

Zoe's eyes were looking into mine now, and I saw a tear making its way down her lips.

"Don't be sad," I said. It seemed like a stupid thing to say, but I meant it. All my life, I'd been grumpy at the sweet, smiley sunflower that was Zoe Hollis. But the only thing worse than her goofy, smiley personality was when it was gone.

"You act like you're this terrible person," she said, holding back the tears. "That's what makes me so sad."

I didn't know what to say.

"But you aren't," said Zoe. "You're kind, and gentle, and you've always looked out for me. Even if you didn't know how. Don't you see?"

I shook my head.

"Adrian, I love you," she said, and the words shattered all the walls I'd built my whole life, and sent them tumbling down at last. And I felt something lighten within myself, and all the worries lift. Even with my business gone, my identity changed, and everything that had happened...

I could fix it all, if I had her.

"I love you too, Zoe," I said, and time seemed to slow down. I looked down at my hands and saw that, just like Zoe's, they were shaking a little.

I've never seen my hands shake. Not once. My professors mentioned it to me in med school, admiring how steady they normally were. *But since when has Zoe Hollis ever made me feel normal?*

I stepped towards her, and I reached out. Zoe put her hands towards me, and they met in the light. There we stood, holding onto one another.

She reached up and kissed me, and I kissed her back, and I felt her hands squeeze mine, until they steadied again. Now, as ever, she brought me a feeling of peace that surpassed everything I'd been through.

"You two are so sweet...." It was Giulia. We both turned, hand in hand. She was standing at the door to the garden. "You know," she said, "I think there's something you forgot to ask."

"Ah," I said. Neither of us had gotten a chance to apologize for not telling her about us.

"Giulia," I began. "I love Zoe. I'm sorry we didn't tell you about us. The truth is," I said, looking apologetically at Zoe, "we didn't really understand until it was too late to tell you. And that was wrong. We ought to have let you know from the start."

Giulia narrowed her eyes.

"But I know to do the right thing," I said. "And I know what Mama would have wanted. And," I said delicately, "with your...*permission*, I'd like to date Zoe."

"Giulia," added Zoe, "I love your brother. It doesn't mean I like you any less. And I'd hate it for things to change between us. You've always been my best friend. Giulia, can we have your permission? To...to be together?"

Giulia thought for a minute, pausing pensively while she put her finger to her lips.

The suspense was agonizing, but eventually, she seemed to think about it, and put her hands down by her sides.

"I'll think about it," she said and went inside.

"I think that means yes," whispered Zoe to me, and then I was kissing her, knowing I'd never let go of her again, and nothing could stop me.

Chapter 27

Zoe

"We're going to miss our flight," I said, breathily, as he placed his arms around my naked shoulders and kissed me once again.

"I don't care," growled Adrian as he held me and I sighed in his arms.

God, I loved it when he spoke to me that way. So commanding and fierce. And I knew, that morning as we tumbled together among the cool, white sheets of his bed, that there was no way I wanted to leave for Italy without another taste of his strength, his muscular heat.

Adrian lowered me back down onto the bed. My body already ached from last night's passion and the night before, but I couldn't care any less. I wanted him again, somehow.

He bent down and kissed my neck, and I felt the tingling feelings of desire course through my body as my hands reached around his bare, strong back. I could feel his shoulder blades and the muscles above undulating as he ran his hands down over my shoulders, towards my bare breasts, and affectionately squeezed them, as one hand gracefully rubbed its thumb over the nipple.

Adrian stayed like that for a little while, his mouth placing gentle kisses on my abdomen while I felt my back arching and moaned a little. "You're teasing me," I moaned, while he stimulated my nipple, and I felt his mouth delicately lingering above the mound of hair.

"Is that right?" he said. "We can't have that."

And then, he lowered himself down to his knees and buried his face deep in my pussy.

The shock of it, of feeling Adrian's mouth there again, hadn't failed to surprise me in the two weeks since we'd got back together. We'd been recovering from our wounds for the first few days. But eventually, we realized that with a month of leave from the hospital after what had happened, there was an even better way to soothe the wounds of those dark, awful times.

And I certainly felt soothed now as he gently sucked at my clit, and started to let his tongue draw slow, gentle circles over it.

I reached down and wrapped my hands in his thick, dark hair. It had grown a little, and I liked it. Looking down to see the thick, dark curls of the man I loved as he looked up and fixed me with a stare sent a shiver of delight down my spine.

I wanted more, and signaled to him, gently tugging on my hair and letting him dutifully rebury his face in my pussy, and I felt his slow, rhythmical pleasuring start to make me quiver. I hooked my legs over his shoulders, and all of a sudden, I was within Adrian's grasp as he pulled my body into him, and I felt myself starting to build towards climax.

"Come here, you," I said, lovingly and lazily dazed by his incredible oral gifts, and Adrian leaped up.

The full force of his muscular, powerful body bent over me. He kissed my neck, harder this time, then continued to bite and caress my skin. I reached for the enormous cock hanging between his legs.

I'm not ashamed to say it. I was still desperate for his cock. I hooked my legs around him and pulled him closer. He knew what I wanted, and was only too happy to oblige, as he spread my legs a little more and pressed the head of his strong, powerful dick against my pussy. I could feel how wet I was for him, and it filled me with excitement. And then, he entered me, a blissful release, and a feeling of safety and security washed over me as Adrian bent down, mounting me and holding me firmly within his grasp.

I sighed and contorted a little, feeling the sheer size of him as he sheathed his cock deep within me. Adrian began to thrust, gently, and as he did, he bent my head up towards him and began to whisper sweet words of passion and delight to my face.

"You're mine," he said. "All mine and I'm never going to let you go."

"That's right," I said. "Oh, Adrian...God, you feel so good. Harder, please?"

"You sure you can take it, princess," he said, arrogantly smiling. I loved it when he played this part for me, of a cruel, dominant masculine man. Now that we knew we loved one another, it was like we were playing a game together, seeing how dirty, desperate, and intense our sex could be, and I leaned back and sighed.

"Give me all you've got."

He began to thrust harder, and it sent sparks of excitement up my spine as I bent and kicked, gasps of longing escaping from my mouth. And then, I felt Adrian's hand guiding my own to my pussy, and began to touch myself a little, stimulating myself on my hand and his delightful, gorgeous manhood as my body began to rise and fall with his, as our breaths met in the air. We both began to shout with the sheer wonderful tingling that I could feel in both our bodies.

Adrian lifted up my legs and brought them around me, and now he was fucking me in the tightest possible position, and I knew what was coming and that there was no way to stop it, that I was his and his alone.

"I'm gonna come," I said. I remembered that Adrian was the first man I'd orgasmed with, the first and last, and the way in which he'd claimed me like that and made me his, only added to the sheer magic of the moment as I felt contractions spreading in my groin. Then I was coming hard for him, harder than I'd ever come before; my desire strengthened, not weakened, by the mess he'd already made of me that week, before I felt him give way and grunt, his mouth opening and his eyes closing with sheer abandon as heat and light descended on me. He filled me, coming equally as hard.

We collapsed together onto the bed, sweating, distracted, utterly dazed by the magic of the encounter. After a few minutes, Adrian sat up, the wavy curls on his forehead distressed and hanging loose around his temples. I bathed in the sheer pleasure of his naked form before me before he bent down and kissed me.

"Come on," he said. "We've got a plane to catch."

*

Luckily, we'd already packed our bags that night, and made it in time for the plane. Giulia was there waiting for us at the airfield.

"I'll never get used to this," she said, shaking her head at us as, hand in hand, we climbed aboard the jet together.

It turns out that when Giulia said she'd 'think about' giving us her permission, she did mean yes. But the yes came with catches. They were presented to us in the form of an A3 colored sheet of sugar paper she'd taken from school, in a light shade of lilac. It was presented to us on the plane, with more than a few love hearts drawn in colorful pink on the side of the paper.

"Terms Under Which Zoe and Adrian Can Have My Permission to Date," said Adrian, and groaned as he picked up the elegantly handwritten list.

"Rule One," I read, as I looked over his shoulder after we'd taken off. "Zoe is Mine on Thursday Nights and Sundays."

"I don't wanna be calling you up and you telling me you're with him," pouted Giulia. "I want you all to myself sometimes. You're my bestie. Besties hang out with besties."

I blushed. "I am your bestie," I said. "So that seems fair."

"Rule Two," said Adrian. "No kissing in front of Giulia."

He wrinkled up his nose. "What, like, ever?"

"Never," she said. "You keep that gross stuff to yourselves. And no funny business in general when I'm around. I'm gonna be in the hotel room next to yours when we get to La Toscana. I better not hear anything!"

"Okay, okay," said Adrian, "it's a deal." But he winked at me, and I giggled, until Giulia fixed us both with a scary look.

"Rule Three," I continued. "Damn, there are a lot of rules here."

"You wanna date my brother?" said Giulia, raising an eyebrow sulkily. "You're gonna obey every one of them, sweetheart. Otherwise, you and me are gonna have some problems! And you," she said, poking a finger threateningly into Adrian's chest. "You're gonna mind your manners from now on. None of this being a grumpy, sulky boy. No more *fuoco*. You're going out with the most beautiful girl in the world," she said, gesturing enthusiastically at me. "So *smile!*"

Adrian did. In fact, he laughed, and so did I. And for the hundredth time that week, I realized how lucky I was to have a best friend like her.

*

Even in the jet, the flight was still long. We eventually arrived at an airfield in Tuscany in the late morning.

When I stepped off the plane, I was dazzled by the look of the landscape. Around us, blue, rolling hills stretched as far as the eye could see. We'd landed on a narrow strip of tarmac in the middle of the countryside, and above us, the sun was already starting to rise.

Adrian had a car waiting to meet us. We were driving to the town of Lucca.

"Lucca?" said Giulia, looking out the window and taking a photo of a particularly unremarkable tree by the side of the road. "As in, us? As in, De Luca?"

"I don't think so," said Adrian. "But who knows?"

We were shocked when we saw the hotel. I knew the hotels in Italy were nice, but Adrian had got us rooms in a five-star place in the *piazza*, the square at the center of town. As we got out, someone rang him on his cellphone.

"Yeah?" said Adrian, and then I saw him stop in the street. His face looked a little tense.

"Is everything okay?" said Giulia, and then she saw her brother was frozen.

"I...I guess, uh...sure," he said.

He put the phone down.

"That was the guy from the Italian consul," he said, breathlessly.

"What did he say?"

"He wants us to go meet someone. A guy named Francesco. Francesco De Luca," he said breathlessly. He looked at Giulia. "Giulia, we've got cousins here. And they want to meet us."

Inside, we hurriedly unpacked. It was 1 pm in the afternoon when we left the hotel, in the car again. Adrian did his best to speak a little Italian, but aside from the few dribs and drabs they'd picked up from their mother, neither of them spoke very much.

"I wonder what they're gonna be like?" said Giulia.

"I don't know," Adrian replied. "Apparently, it's a big family. De Luca's an old name in Italy. It's from this part of the world. They're looking up our relatives and were calling a few people in the area. But apparently, these are the only people who recognized our names and the dates when we disappeared."

"Oh my God," said Giulia. "Is...is he gonna be there?"

Adrian shook his head. "That was my first question."

I could see his fist clench next to me in the car, the knuckles whitening. I put my own hand over it, and he looked up at me and smiled. But I could see he still burned inwardly at the thought of his uncle, the man who had planned it all.

It was mid-afternoon and the sun had already begun to sink a little in the sky by the time we came off the highway and pulled up a short, bumpy dirt road. At the crest of the green hill, framed by the Apennine mountains, I could see a villa. It was a square, wide marble building, and as we approached it, I could see the place had an enormous wooden gate.

"Wow," said Giulia. "Look."

We were now passing through a grove of olive trees and stopping at the top of the hill. We got out. In the distance, I thought I heard the chatter of voices and the sound of music.

Then, from inside the courtyard at the front of the villa, I saw a plump man approaching us. His skin was bronzed and leathery, and he wore a wide, white shirt. On top of his head was a wispy crop of white hair and rough stubble. He must have been in his seventies at least. He looked the picture of an old-school mafia don. Except for the fact that he was jolly, and grinning as he approached us and spoke in a hoarse, husky voice.

"*Buon giorno!*" said the man, and threw his arms up. "Adriano! Giuliana!"

He approached and embraced them, kissing them on their cheeks. "And this is Zoe, *si?*"

"Are you Francesco?" said Adrian, as the jolly man shook my hand.

"*Si*, I am he," chuckled the man. "And you! *Bambino*. It has been thirty years since I last see you. You are looking so strong. All the men in this family are strong! And *madamina*," he said, clasping Giulia around the shoulders. "So beautiful. I always say, the women in this family. So beautiful! *Bella ragazza!*"

I'd never seen Giulia blush any more than in this moment, but Adrian looked dumbfounded.

"I've met you before?" he said.

"Si! I come and hold you. When you are a...'ow you say? A *baby*," he said. "You are, I say to my wife, the most beautiful boy. We think," he said, "that you die in the fire, along with your poor *mamma*."

"But, who are you?" said Adrian.

"I am your father's cousin. So I am a your third cousin. Cousin

Francesco, you call me. Come on. Come on."

"This is a beautiful house," said Adrian, as Francesco led us across the courtyard.

"We grow olive trees here," he said. "We have grown them for twenty generations."

"Wow," said Giulia.

"This is incredible," I said. In the distance, I could hear chattering.

"What's that noise?" Adrian said.

"Everyone is-a waiting here to meet you," said Francesco.

"Everyone?" said Adrian.

"Everyone," repeated Francesco as we rounded a corner. The site blew me away.

Over the terrace, someone had hung a banner. It read: *Adriano é Giuliana*. Below the banner, on the terrace in the sunshine, stood a crowd of about thirty Italians. Little children, dressed up smartly in waistcoats and shorts. Fashionable men and women, wearing Armani suits and sunglasses, elegant and handsome. And old nonnas and grandpas. A swell, a roar, of excitement took over, and suddenly we were thronged by people, greeting us, shaking our hands, kissing our cheeks.

"*Ciao!*"

"*Paola! Bambini di Stefano* (You are Stefano's children?)! *Adriano!*"

They crowded around us, shaking our hands, holding us. And before we knew it, we were all of us in tears. But no one more so than Giulia.

"I thought it was just us," she kept saying. "All these years, I thought it was just us two."

*

We were immediately served lunch together, and I gathered they'd been waiting for us to get started. Francesco and his wife, Andrea, spoke a little English, as did their son, Alfredo, and his wife, Carlotta.

"But please to say," she said to me, "what is your name?"

"Zoe," I said. I loved saying hello to them. Everyone here was so friendly and talkative that I hardly felt out of place. I was instantly myself among Adrian's family, not too shy nor too talkative.

"Ah, *Zoe!*" she said. "What a beautiful name! You are to be married to Adrian?"

"I...I don't know," I said. I looked at him, Adrian, happily talking with the guests. "We hadn't even begun to think about it." But I knew I would say yes without any hesitation.

"But you are friends with Giuliana, yes?"

"Oh, yeah," I said, beaming and looking over at her as a gaggle of kids surrounded her. "Best friends"

How could I explain to these people what Adrian and Giulia had meant to me? That we'd been together since we were children? That I'd wanted Adrian for the longest time and always thought it would never happen.

"It was one of the greatest tragedies. We thought Adriano and Giulia were dead. And Estella. Stefano's wife. She was well-liked. We are sorry to hear she's gone."

"Me too," I said. I thought of Estella then, far away from her friends and family, making a new life for her children. She'd made the ultimate sacrifice to keep them safe. It reminded me again what a good person she was.

"But what do you mean?" said Francesco. "You are the heir to the property?"

"I know," said Adrian. "Trouble is, I don't know where it is."

"The...?" said Francesco, and then said something to his wife. "Ah. *Mi dispiace.* I am sorry. I do not understand. Where it is? What do you mean?"

Adrian shrugged. "I don't know. *Dov'é?*" The Italian word for where. I listened with anticipation as Francesco puzzled over the question. Eventually, he shook his head and chuckled.

"*Adriano*, the estate is all around us!"

"All around?" said Adrian.

"Your grandfather's father," he said slowly. "After the war. He built hospitals, yes?"

"Hospitals?" said Adrian.

"*Si.* And these hospitals, well, there are twenty, or maybe twenty-five of these hospitals, all over *Toscana. That* is your birthright, Adriano. That is your inheritance. You belong to one of Italy's greatest medical families."

"And my father?"

"Your papa, he was a doctor like you. I will send you tomorrow. But for now," he said, smiling, "*Familia.* And wine!"

Chapter 28

Adrian

We got home late that night from a riotous party, full of songs and happiness. But even though it was good to be among relatives that Giulia and I had thought would be lost forever, I still knew that somewhere, out there in the darkness, the man was waiting. The man who'd wronged my family. My uncle, Giovanni De Luca.

That night, I made a few calls. It was late in the day to be calling officials in Italy, most of whom didn't run twenty-four-hour offices. But, at 3 in the morning, while Zoe was still sleeping, I awoke to the sound of my phone ringing.

"Is that Doctor Adrian Lawson?"

"Yes," I said. "Who is this?"

"My name is Mister Francesci. I'm driving up from Rome to meet you. Which hotel are you staying at?"

"The Bella Ponte, in Lucca."

"Excellent. You are going to the Hospital Santa Maria tomorrow?"

"That's right," I said.

"Very good. I will meet you at your hotel. Let us say 9:30 am?"

"Okay," I said, and put the phone down.

Even though I was tired, from the long flight and the longer party, I didn't sleep another wink that night. My head was too full of strange thoughts and a feeling of foreboding.

The following morning, I got out of bed and got dressed. I headed to the lobby of the hotel and had a cup of coffee. There, I met Francesci. Like everyone I'd seen around here so far, he was dressed elegantly in a dark blue suit and a smart, silk tie.

He shook my hand. "I have notified the relevant authorities," he said.

"Then I guess we should go," I said, rubbing my eyes.

We got up and went to the front door of the hotel.

Then, behind me, I heard Zoe's voice.

"Wait! Adrian!" she said. I turned around. "Where are you going?" she asked, walking towards me. She'd pulled on her clothes. I hadn't wanted Zoe to go with me, fearing what we might find at the hospital.

"Hospital Santa Maria," I explained.

"Why?" she said, confused.

I shrugged. "To finish this."

Zoe folded her arms and narrowed her eyes. She wasn't the same person I'd met a few months ago. The woman in front of me was determined to see this through by my side. I didn't even think about saying no when she said, "I'm going with you."

*

The hospital was an hour's drive out of town, but it served as the main hospital for the local area. I'd had a car pick us up from the hotel, and now as we rode along through the dazzling, sunny countryside, I looked at Zoe. She was staring out of the window. If she was scared, she didn't show it.

"You don't have to come inside if you don't want to."

She looked at me and smiled.

"I'm not letting you go anywhere without me again," she said. "You do realize that, right? From now on, whatever we do, we do as a team."

I smiled and squeezed her hand. In the passenger's seat up front, Francesci said nothing as we crested one of the hills outside of Lucca and began to make our way into the mountains.

The hospital was sleek and modern, an enormous building with a glass front set high up in the hills. It was the first point of contact for people being emergency-lifted out of the mountains. I'd read up a bit on it last night, and it seemed like any hospital around the world. The glossy website showed airbrushed images of doctors and nurses, state-of-the-art machinery, and clean, sanitized surfaces. But the Hospital Santa Maria was the flagship of the De Luca trust, which managed hospitals all over Italy catering to specialist medical needs and housing state-of-the-art surgeries.

And its director was my uncle. The man who'd tried to have me killed and kidnapped Zoe. Giovanni De Luca.

As we approached the enormous, steel-and-glass structure, I looked around me nervously.

"Where are the others?" I said to Francesci.

"They are here," he said, confidently. "Waiting for us."

When we made our way through the hospital gates and began

to drive up the steep incline to the front entrance, I made a phone-call.

"We're here," I said.

"About time," replied a familiar voice. "I've been here for hours."

It was Duncan Reed. The Private Investigator.

We got out and went inside the hospital, and I saw him, waiting by the lobby. We shook hands. "Thanks for coming out here, Duncan," I said.

"Wouldn't miss it for the world," he replied.

"You have the photograph?" Francesci said to Duncan.

"I do," he said, and reached into his bag.

The police had confiscated Duncan's camera and the photos he'd taken for me while I'd employed him to track Paul and Detective Vance. But Duncan was smart. He backed up everything to external servers from his office. Out of the plain, dark sports bag he had around his shoulder, he produced a copy of the photograph he'd shown me weeks ago: detective Vance, meeting with Giovanni, just outside of Cañon. As he passed it to Francesci, I looked at the face of the old man. But I didn't need to. I'd recognize him anywhere. His face was imprinted on my mind.

We went to the reception desk. Francesci kindly translated for me.

"I'm the Doctor, from America," I said. "Adrian Lawson. I asked to come visit Giovanni De Luca and see the hospital."

Francesci repeated the words in Italian to the receptionist, who nodded and pulled up her calendar on a wide, silver screen.

"Mister De Luca will see you now," she said in Italian and

Francesci translated. "Please take the elevator to the top floor."

As we went into the elevator and I pushed the button, Francesci pulled his wrist up to his mouth and whispered something. I noticed the earpiece in his ear and suddenly realized that he was more prepared than I thought he was. He gave off the impression of a quiet, emotionless functionary. But Francesci wasn't just anyone. He was one of the senior investigators in Italy's branch of Interpol, specializing in fraud and white-collar crime.

After what seemed like forever, the elevator finally arrived at the hospital's top floor. We stepped out into a plush, expensive-looking lobby, decorated with dark wood paneling and humming quietly with activity. Personal assistants and admin staff walked around us, chatting in Italian. Unlike what I'd seen from the rest of the country, the people were quiet, subdued. They knew that something was up with our sudden arrival.

At the desk, we signed in and were shown into a meeting room. It was a beautiful room, with dark blue wallpaper and an enormous, heavy wooden table in the center. Zoe and I took our seats at one end, flanked by Reed and Francesci. We waited there in the stillness.

"No one is to do anything until I say," said Francesci, and we nodded.

"What if he's got something planned for us?" said Duncan, and the inspector chuckled. It was a thin, dry laugh, and after he'd finished, he resumed his stony, passive expression.

"This is Italy," he said. "Even the criminals will act like gentlemen. And, besides," he said, tapping his breast pocket gently. "I do not come unprepared."

I felt the hairs on the back of my neck stand up. We all knew what he meant. I reached out to put my hand on Zoe's, and she looked at me. Between us, we were developing a private code, a secret way of talking to one another. The look in her eyes meant: *I trust you.* She was glad to be here with me at the end of it all.

There was the sound of a door slamming and a low, steady voice drawling in Italian. Slowly, we watched as two men in suits came down past the glass window. Behind them, following on, was a face I'd only seen in grainy, black-and-white up until now.

I was struck by how much his face resembled Wesley, a little thinner than my own but the same basic shape. His nose was turned up as he approached us. He dressed in a double-breasted suit, old-fashioned looking, but with no tie. Instead, he had a cravat tied around his neck. He looked like any well-to-do Florentine or Italian gentleman. But on his cheek was a scar, raised a little.

I knew what that scar meant. Or at least, I thought I knew what it meant now. It was called a *sfregio*. A gang symbol. A slash across the face meant that the wearer was marked for life as indebted to a gang. I guess there might have been a lot of reasons that Giovanni had done what he'd done. But when I saw his eye imperiously fix on me, I knew that one of them was certainly fear. Fear of losing the comfortable life he had here, and the wealth he'd accumulated.

He entered the room with his flunkies.

"Good morning, gentlemen," he said, and a slow smile spread across his face. But the expression in his eyes didn't change. It was like making eye contact with a dangerous predator. I wanted to avert my eyes, but forced myself to hold his gaze.

I stood, and extended a hand. "Mister De Luca," I said, but he waved his hand.

"I know who you are, young man," he said brusquely. "And I know who it is you claim to be."

I said nothing, but stood there.

"Who is it you think I claim to be."

"You claim to be Adriano De Luca," he said, softly. "You are claiming, under false pretenses, to be the eldest son of my dear, departed sister-in-law, Estella De Luca. You *claim*," he said, in his thick, musical accent, "to be the heir to the business I inherited."

"Your son Paul De Luca's confirmed that already," said Duncan Reed, who was simmering in tension next to me. Just like me, he wanted to see Giovanni punished for his crimes.

"Please," said Giovanni, and turned to Francesci. "You see how preposterous this is? This arrogant American is coming to our country and telling me that it is my fault because my son has committed a crime. I'm not responsible for what Paul does," he said, grinning. "He has always been a disappointment to the family."

Right there, in his words, I could see how Paul De Luca had been turned into the monster he was. Giovanni had twisted his life and made him feel inferior, belittling him. Meeting the father finally helped me understand why the son was the way he was.

"You're going to let your own son take the blame?" said Zoe. "That's awful."

Giovanni snorted. "I can see now it was wrong to even agree to meet you. I had hoped to put your suspicions to rest. But if you think you can blackmail me out of my hospital, then you have another thing coming."

"Mister De Luca," said Francesci, quietly, and then asked him a question in Italian.

"*Non*," said Giovanni.

"I just asked him if he has been to the United States recently," he said. "I am now going to show him the photograph."

"Since you have not been out of the country in the last three months, Mister De Luca, can you identify the man in this picture for me?"

He took Duncan's photo and slid it across the table. Giovanni didn't even look down at first. Then, slowly, his eyes traveled downwards, and he studied the picture.

We heard his breathing grow a little faster.

"That isn't me," said Giovanni, angrily. "That isn't me at all!"

But his words sounded hollow even as they came out of his mouth. Giovanni turned and snapped at one of his advisors, who picked up the photograph and looked at it. They hadn't expected this.

"You," said Giovanni, standing up and gesturing at me. "Get out."

"Mister De Luca," said Francesci, in a dull monotone, and then began to speak lowly and slowly in Italian. But I could pick out the words—*arrest, warrant, extradition.*

Snarling, Giovanni cursed and picked up a water glass. He turned and left the room.

"Arrest him," said Francesci, again, into his earpiece.

Then, all hell broke loose.

The police had been waiting on the stairwell outside. Plainclothes officers came onto the floor and began shouting. In the confusion, I grabbed Zoe, and we laid down on the ground under the table while the shouting and banging continued. Eventually, the noises came to a stop, and then we heard Giovanni, swearing and screaming, begging to be let go.

Once he'd been arrested, Giovanni De Luca was taken to a local police station in Florence. Embarrassed at the whole situation and under pressure from the U.S. Ambassador, he was extradited to the United States. He was charged with conspiracy to commit murder, kidnapping, and fraud. For which he'd likely face a jail sentence of up to thirty years once convicted.

It was the first and last time I'd ever met my uncle.

*

Then began a whole new round of questioning, by the Italian *polizie*. How long had I known Giovanni? When had I become aware of him? It was like I was answering all of the same questions again. Except this time, I was even less certain of the answers.

It turned out that when I'd mentioned Giovanni De Luca and told the police I had the means to prosecute him, they hadn't just jumped on it for my own sake. Giovanni was suspected of having links to organized crime groups in the area. My uncle had been paying off debts to the mob for a long time. Francesci explained all this to me after we drove back from Florence, where Zoe, Duncan, and I had spent most of the day being interrogated.

It was late by the time we arrived at Lucca, and all the lights were off. The town looked a little more eerie at night, with its angular skylines and lamps lit on the sides of the buildings, like something out of a movie.

"Is this gonna make the papers?" I said.

He looked at me. "I think so, yes," he said.

"Will I be safe? Will *we* be safe?"

He nodded. "No one is coming after you. Your uncle, though. If the police want to make him talk about the gangs, about the *mafia*...he may be in trouble."

I shuddered at the thought of what will happen to Giovanni. Then realized that I didn't really care about him. Not after what he'd done to me and my sister, my mother. Out of purely selfish motivations, too.

We were dropped off at the hotel and bid goodnight by Francesci. It was still and dark, and the night was hot.

"Are you hungry?" I said.

"No," replied Zoe. "Just worried."

"About what?"

"About you. You seem so sad at the moment. And today was so scary. It made me think about the warehouse. About Paul."

I nodded and put my arms around her. I drew Zoe into an embrace.

"I guess I am sad," I said. "About what might have been?"

"You mean if your mother hadn't had to leave?"

"If my father hadn't died."

"Your father loved you, Adrian."

"I've lost so much of my family. I might have grown up here if it weren't for Giovanni."

"Then you never would have met me," said Zoe, absentmindedly. But I caught her chin and tilted her head up to meet my eyeline.

"Then I'm glad I didn't," I said. "I'm glad I'm here with you."

The church bell tolled midnight, and we kissed in the square. Around us, the streetlamps glowed, and for the first of many times, I realized how much lighter the world was with Zoe Hollis in it.

Chapter 29

Zoe

"No! Come on. We were only gone for a day!"

Shocked, I grabbed onto Giulia's arm, and we giggled the same way we'd been giggling since we were fourteen years old.

Adrian had gone to take care of something, but he'd arranged for us to meet him at a fancy restaurant in town. It was getting hotter, almost the middle of summer now, and we were happy to be at a table under a leafy, green tree whose shade covered us with a pleasing cool breeze.

"Who is he?"

"I met him yesterday while I was out shopping."

"You went shopping without me?"

"Well, looks like I missed the fun, huh? What was he like? Our uncle?"

"Scary," I said, trying to brush off the events of yesterday. "So, come on," I said. "Tell me."

"Tell you what?" said Giulia, coyly.

"What's his name?"

"His name?" said Giulia, raising an eyebrow. "Okay, think of the sexiest, sexy Italian guy-sounding name you can think of."

"Uh...*Carlo*," I said, rolling the 'r' as I said it, and Giulia laughed and shook her head.

"No!"

The waiter arrived with a bottle of white wine while I thought again.

"Um...how about...*Gino*," I said, doing my best to imitate the exaggerated emphasis on the first syllable.

"No!" she said. "But you're on the right track."

"Okay," I said, taking a sip of my wine and leaning back to look down the cobbled street we were sitting on: *Sun, wine, and beautiful little towns with cobbled streets. I could get used to this.*

After a while, I gave up. "It's hopeless," I said. "I don't know."

"*Lorenzo*," said Giulia, and we broke into laughter together. It was infectious between us, and always had been. When one of us laughed, the other couldn't help but join in.

"Lorenzo!" I said. "Is he handsome?"

"Oh, he's *beautiful*," said Giulia. "A real Italian stallion!" She did a mock heroic pose, flexing her biceps.

"Where's he taking you?"

"Where every cultured Italian goes on a Friday night, Zoe. The opera."

"The opera? That's incredible!" I was so happy for Giulia. "Have you got a good feeling?"

"You know, I kind of do. He's like, handsome. And good-looking. If only we weren't leaving tomorrow," she said, sadly.

248

Adrian had offered to let Zoe and I stay for another week, but it was time for him to go home and face the music. He was going to have to appeal to the U.S. Treasury to get his money back. It turned out that, while Adrian and Giulia were both U.S. citizens and had their citizenship guaranteed, Adrian's business was in a different situation. He'd had hundreds of investors pull out after the revelations, and even though he had more money than he could ever spend in a lifetime, his business days in New York were over. I knew my place was by his side, and I had to go back with him. The next few weeks would be hard. The hospital had also suspended Adrian, and it didn't look like he'd be able to practice medicine again until his name had been cleared. Which, of course, wouldn't happen until Giovanni, Paul, and Vance were behind bars.

"What are you two giggling about?" said Adrian from behind us. He leaned down and kissed my cheek.

"Yuck!" said Giulia.

"Be nice," said Adrian. "Besides, I hear somebody made a date for this afternoon."

"You..." said Giulia, before she turned to me and glared. "You told him!"

"Well, of course I told him!" I said.

"I'm glad she did," Adrian said, as he sat down. He was dressed in a white linen shirt and a pair of tan pants, and under the tree, he took off his Raybans and revealed his deep, dark eyes. I shuddered momentarily with desire for him.

"Oh man," Giulia whined. "Now he's gonna be all, 'What time are you getting home?' and 'Who is this jerk anyhow?'" she said, making fun of Adrian's deep voice as she did. "You remember how he was when you used to go out with other guys?"

"What?" I said, and felt my cheeks flush.

"Oh, come on," said Adrian, defensively.

"You're kidding, right?" said Giulia. "He hounded me for details about the guys, socials, numbers, university student IDs. Now it makes sense why."

"Is that true?" I said.

"Of course it is!" said Giulia. She was acting like we were stupid. "He always hated all those stupid guys you went out with in college. And remember that time in the club?"

"What time?" we said, almost in unison. But we both remembered.

"He's a chauvinist. Plain and simple."

"Well, I think he's a gentleman," I said, a little bashfully.

"A little of both?" said Adrian, and we laughed and chinked our glasses.

*

Luckily, since Adrian had decided to come to Italy, they were able to return his Lamborghini to him there. Among other things, he'd been picking it up that morning. Together, we sailed through the Tuscan hills with the top down. The beautiful vistas sailed past us as we drove up and out of the valley.

Together, at last. Just the two of us. As we climbed higher and higher into the mountains, I felt we were leaving behind the shadows of the past.

"Do you like it out here?" said Adrian.

"I do," I said. "I mean, I love it."

He nodded. "Me too. You know, Zoe, my family's here. I'd

never want to take you away from yours, but I think I'm going to have to spend some more time out here. Would you like to come with me when I return?"

I looked at him. My dark, masculine, handsome man. My gorgeous, wealthy doctor. I'd follow him to the ends of the earth if I had to. I'd live anywhere he wanted. I certainly wouldn't say no to coming back to Italy with him.

"So, what happens now?" I said. "With the hospitals? With the De Luca estate?"

"With the absence of a legitimate heir," he said, "it falls into trustee ownership. But my mother's diary holds the key. Once we get that back...this could all be mine and Giulia's."

"Wow," I said. "It looks like you're gonna still be working in business after all."

Adrian nodded and looked thoughtful. "You know, having my financial stuff in New York and working in a hospital never really made sense to me. Like the two weren't connected. But here, if I do make a claim for the estate...I can combine my love for the two."

"You'll have to learn Italian," I said.

"Hey, I speak plenty Italian!"

"Not enough to be a doctor here," I said.

"Not right now. But I can learn. I can put my mind to anything if I try."

"You're incredible."

"Come off it."

"I mean it. Look at what you've been through. You're not just a survivor, Adrian. You've made the best of things wherever you are. Whoever you're with."

"I can do a whole lot better now I'm with you," he said, and I felt that delightful warm feeling in my chest, the ache which I'd hidden for so long. But now I didn't have to anymore.

"I love you," I told him.

"I love you too," he said. "There it is!"

I looked up, following his gaze up the hillside.

And then, I saw it.

A simple, white house. A wrought iron gate around the front. And a sloping, terracotta roof. It stood above a little copse of trees, just up the hill from where we were.

"What's that?" I said.

Adrian remained quiet, and we drove up to the villa. We pulled off a side road and drove up through the trees, green and leafy, lush even at this altitude.

"I had them open it up for us," explained Adrian as we pulled up and got out of our car. "Come on. Let's go look inside."

It was like a dream. The most wonderful, pleasant dream I'd had. We passed through the white archway of the house to its central courtyard. In the middle, a stone fountain revealed a leaping school of fish, water spouting from their mouths.

"This place is incredible," I said.

"Will it do?" said Adrian.

I stopped and turned to him.

"Do for what?" I said.

He smiled and laughed. I still had to get used to Adrian laughing. When he was a teenager, I'd hardly ever seen him laugh. He was always so moody that it was strange to see the shadow lifting from his face.

"You always underestimate yourself," he said. "I've never liked that. You think it's nice for me to have you, to be around you. But it's more than that, Zoe. I couldn't be without you. And I couldn't imagine sharing a place this beautiful with anyone but you."

"Adrian. Is this...for us?"

He looked at me. "I guess it is," he said and smiled that dark, confident smile of his that I've loved since the moment I met him.

"To live here?"

"For a while. Not forever. But we'll need somewhere to stay while I'm here sorting things out. With my father's estate."

I turned and looked around at the high walls surrounding the courtyard. It wasn't ostentatious, though the house was pretty big. It was simple and perfect and beautiful, with space enough for...for, well, whatever we wanted.

"Are you going to make an offer?" I said.

"The offer's here," said Adrian, and I turned around.

He was on one knee, in the courtyard. The air was humming with the heat, and in the distance, I could hear wind rolling through the hills.

Adrian had a tiny, dark box in his hands. He opened it and showed me its contents.

Inside, there was something tiny and delicate, winking at me in the sunlight.

"What...what's that?" I said. I was shaking, my whole body was shaking. I could feel the sunlight on me and it seemed to only agitate my pounding heart.

"It's a ring," said Adrian.

We were silent together, me standing, him, the man of my dreams, below me. And beyond him, out through a gap in the courtyard, wide, rolling mountainside, stretching all the way down into the valley.

"Zoe," said Adrian. "Will you...?"

I was speechless.

"Will you marry me?" said Adrian.

In the sky, I could see the wings of a bird. Caught between heart-rending nerves and a feeling of utter peace, I watched it, circling on the breeze.

It took a plunge out of sight, down the mountainside.

I took a deep breath. And thought about a long, hot summer, sixteen years ago.

"Yes. In this lifetime and the next."

Epilogue

Zoe

7 months later...

It was spring, and I was back there, in the courtyard.

Because ever since then, I'd been waiting. Waiting to take the next step in the remarkable, wonderful life I've been privileged to have.

Not everything had been perfect, of course, and the lingering effects of the past have made themselves known.

At night, sometimes, especially when I was at home in Cañon, I woke up in my bed, my heart pounding and the ceiling swirling above me. It was normal, of course. And my doctor said I was doing remarkably well after I was attacked and kidnapped. I was one of the lucky ones, I guess. Maybe it was my optimism, which reminded me that in the end everything turned out okay. Better than okay.

But I think it was really the fact that, if I ever had bad dreams, or was ever reminded of those dark, terrible days when I thought everything was lost, I knew that next to me slept the strongest man I'd ever known. A man who'd had to face truths just as harsh, who risked it all for my sake. Who saved my life in more ways than one.

Because the thing about being smiley, happy Zoe Hollis was that sometimes, you didn't feel like being smiley. Sometimes, you liked to cry. To let off a little steam. Sometimes the unfairness of it all made you angry.

But everyone has those days. The difference with me was that I picked myself up and carried on.

Even when the road was hard. Even when the journey was long.

But today was a special day. And, as I stood in the courtyard with my dad, I realized that I wasn't just saying hello to a future. I was saying goodbye to that past.

Because this is the place where I spent those years heading to.

And now, an old, antique white car was pulling up at the front of the villa, and we were getting in, and it was all starting to happen so fast I could barely keep up. Our destination? A tiny, local church just a few miles down the road.

Today was the day I was marrying Adrian Lawson.

I supposed soon his name would be Adrian De Luca. But I didn't want to take the surname he was born with; the surname he'd only just realized was his. I wanted to take the name of the man I grew up with. He was the man I fell in love with, the man I always wanted.

At the church, which had been decorated in sweet-smelling spring flowers, we stopped outside.

My dad looked around and squeezed my hand.

"I am so proud of you," he said, and I smiled at him and hugged him.

"Dad," I said. "Tell me the truth. Do I look ridiculous?"

"Well," he says, grinning. "You sure don't look the same way you did when you came out here earlier this year. But you know, sweetheart? I think you look beautiful. And I know he does, too."

He checked his watch. "We're late," he said, and together, we stepped inside.

One thing no one ever tells you about getting married is that when you enter, and everyone stands, it's such a shock. It's a shock to know that so many people love you, care about you, and want to be with you on this day.

And now I was getting to see them all. Today was a day to thank them.

Together, we passed through the crowd, and in the rafters of the church, I could hear music, sweet music, coming down all around us.

Smiling faces everywhere. Friends and relations had come all the way from Colorado to be here. Adrian and Giulia's family were here, all the relatives who could be drawn from around Italy to come and see. Meeting his mother's people has been special too. It turns out that Estella wasn't from Tuscany but was actually a Southerner. In the end, Adrian's family had filled the aisles to the point where they'd needed to put extra chairs out for them.

I passed my mom, and she smiled at me and waved. Adrian and Megan, my mom, made up the last time we were back in Cañon City for Christmas. She apologized for ever doubting him, and he gracefully accepted her apology, with one of his own in turn. When she found out we were engaged, my mother frowned.

"While I'm overjoyed to hear the news," she said, "I am concerned we'll have to let one of you go. After all, I can't exactly let one of the doctors marry the nurses."

It turned out that she might lose both of us. Once the cases against Giovanni, Paul and Vance had finished and they had been given lengthy jail sentences, and we got back the evidence to prove Adrian's legitimacy, Adrian had started working in Italy almost immediately. Once he'd learned the language, he formally stated his claim for the estate, and since there were no objections, it was looking like the hospitals would pass into his hands. He'd decided to qualify as a doctor in Italy before he started learning the business, though. It was a long process. It could take a lot of time before Adrian was ready to take on the running of the hospitals. That was good, though. We both knew it would be difficult to uproot and move to Italy straightaway, and it was nice to have an excuse to come back to Cañon.

Except that pretty soon, I wasn't going to be working.

There was one slight snag on this whole, perfect day, and it's that I didn't have my first choice of wedding dress. Almost as soon as Adrian and I had announced we were engaged, Giulia took me shopping for one. It was beautiful, a vintage dress made in New York in the 1990s. I'd never seen something so wonderful, and it fitted me perfectly.

And then, the next month, I realized something was up.

My periods come like clockwork—I'm lucky that way. And so I knew, when I missed the first one, what had happened. Almost immediately.

But it was only when I missed the second that I faced facts. I was going to need to see a doctor. Now, I was just a month away from my due date.

I wish I could tell you I was frustrated, annoyed, about the fact that I wasn't going to be able to work. I wish I could tell you that I was worried.

But I am *only* excited. I am *only* delighted. Okay, I admit it. I'm a little terrified. Over the course of the past 7 months, the little life inside of me had grown, and things had changed. Adrian had changed. He was somehow more peaceful, less moody. And yet, he was more determined than he'd ever been. We both knew that his life, without a father, wasn't always the easiest one. And he was determined to be the best father he could be.

On the left-hand side, beyond the crowd, I saw Giulia. There wasn't even anyone else close in the running to be my maid of honor. Only, she wasn't so fond of the title. "I'm not a maid," she said, pursing her lips when I floated it to her. "Can't I be a babe of honor, instead?"

She was still her funny, old self. But these days, I noticed Giulia was getting sentimental. I came into her house last Winter for a catch-up and heard a bunch of soppy love songs on the stereo.

We all knew what was going on. But Giulia was a woman who could never be rushed. We had to wait for her to tell us what was going on. And I felt lucky to be the person she confided in first.

"I love him," she said. "I love Lorenzo. I call him all the time, and we talk about how much we miss each other. And he's in Italy, and I'm here, and...*ARGH*! It's terrible! Terrible, Zoe!"

I gave her a hug and told her things would be okay. For once, I felt like I was justified in telling her not to worry. After all, I'd gone through so much to be with Adrian.

But in the Spring, when we came down to Italy to get ready for the wedding, we brought Giulia with us.

And Lorenzo was waiting for her at the airport with an engagement ring of her own. He was sitting in the front row right now, beaming up at her. He was at least a foot shorter than her. I'll never understand that girl.

"Trust me, Zoe," she told me one morning at breakfast. "What he lacks in height..."

She gave me an ominous look, and I almost spat out my coffee when I realized what she was talking about. "Giulia! Let's *please* move on," I said, quickly.

So Giulia, too, was happy and determined to move to Italy as soon as possible.

And then, through the parting in the crowd, I saw him.

Adrian was wearing a white linen suit for the day. It was the kind of flamboyant, elegant thing he'd do. When he saw me, I noticed his eyes sparkle and knew that, even if I wasn't walking down here in the dress I planned to wear, he still thought I was beautiful. Perhaps even more beautiful.

At night, when it had been getting a little colder, he'd taken to building a fire in the spacious living room of our getaway home up here in the Tuscan hills. He likes to sit with me by the fire. It's his favorite thing to do now. Rather than trading on stocks or whiling the night away reading some obscure medical journal, he prefers to sit with me and talk to me. And to the baby.

As I got there, at last, Adrian stepped down and shook hands with my father.

And then, at last, as people took their seats, we were here, at the place we'd wanted to be. The vows came by, and we recited them. Promising to be with one another always. Promising to always love and take care of one another. Promises we'd made a thousand times over to ourselves but were now making in this special place, in front of the people we loved.

And then, somehow, I was saying *I do*. And then, in the heady blur of that moment, the moment I'd been waiting for all my life, Adrian leaned towards me and took me in his arms and kissed me.

"I love you," he said.

"I love you too," I replied. In the end, it was all that mattered. All that we needed to make that long, slow, wonderful journey on through life, past the places we had been, towards the places we were going.

- THE END -

OTHER SERIES' BY THE AUTHOR

Billionaire Daddy Series

A riveting collection of 5 standalone, fade-to-black, two hour reads.

Mountain Man Daddy Series

A heart throbbing collection of 4 standalone, steamy, three hour reads.

Hadsan Cove Series

A heartwarming collection of 4 standalone, steamy, three hour reads. Best part...you'll get to experience each and every couple's milestones as the main characters become secondary characters in the next book.

Mafia Billionaire Daddy Series

An edge-of-your-seat bundle of 3 standalone, spicy novels.

Printed in Great Britain
by Amazon

33497110R00157